Claudia Talks About: Shoplifting

My best friend Jody has a new hobby—shoplifting! She takes something new almost every day. I'm really worried about her—what if she gets caught? Jody says I shouldn't make a big deal about it. She says lots of kids shoplift. But I know stealing is wrong. My parents taught me that, before they died.

My name is Claudia Salinger. You've probably heard about my family. Everyone at school knows the story. We live alone in my house—just my brothers, my sister, and I.

My parents died in a car accident a little over two years ago, when I was ten. That's when my oldest brother, Charlie, became our legal guardian. He's twenty-five, so I guess everyone figured he was old enough to take care of us. But sometimes he really messes things up. Like the time he forgot to pay the electric bill. We lived in the dark for a week!

But it's okay when Charlie makes a mistake. Bailey is always there to fix it. He's my other big brother. He's in college, and he's the coolest. Whenever I have a problem, I ask Bailey for help. Like when I'm afraid I might forget how my parents' voices sounded. Or how they looked. Bailey says my brothers and sister will always be there to help me remember.

My sister, Julia, reminds me of my mother sometimes. She's really smart and pretty, like Mom was. Julia is in high school. I want to be just like her when I'm seventeen!

Then there's Owen. He's only two and a half. But I can tell that someday he's going to be a brain surgeon or something. He already knows how to spell my name with his blocks. He's *so* smart. I think he takes after me!

My brothers and sister are always busy with school or work or girlfriends and boyfriends. And I'm always busy practicing my violin. I love playing—it reminds me of my mom. Charlie says I inherited her talent. Mom used to play with one of the best orchestras in the country. Maybe one day I'll do the same thing.

Sometimes we get so busy that we don't see one another enough. That's why we eat dinner together at least once a week. We go to Salinger's, the restaurant my dad used to own. They always have our table reserved—for a party of five.

Claudia

PARTY OF FIVE™: Claudia

Welcome to My World
Too Cool for School
A Boy Friend Is Not a "Boyfriend"
The Best Things in Life Are Free. Right?

party of five

Claudia

The Best Things in
Life Are Free. Right?

Page McBrier

**Based on the television series
created by Christopher Keyser
& Amy Lippman**

A
MINSTREL®
BOOK

Published by POCKET BOOKS
New York   London   Toronto   Sydney   Tokyo   Singapore

This book is a work of fiction. Names, characters, places and incidents are products of the author's imagination or are used fictitiously. Any resemblance to actual events or locales or persons, living or dead, is entirely coincidental.

A MINSTREL PAPERBACK *Original*

 A Minstrel Book published by
POCKET BOOKS, a division of Simon & Schuster Inc.
1230 Avenue of the Americas, New York, NY 10020

A PARACHUTE PRESS BOOK

Copyright © 1997 by Columbia Pictures Television, Inc. All Rights Reserved.

Columbia Pictures Television is a SONY PICTURES ENTERTAINMENT Company.

All rights reserved, including the right to reproduce this book or portions thereof in any form whatsoever. For information address Pocket Books, 1230 Avenue of the Americas, New York, NY 10020

ISBN: 0-671-00682-7

First Minstrel Books printing May 1997

10 9 8 7 6 5 4 3 2 1

PARTY OF FIVE and its characters are trademarks of Columbia Pictures Television, Inc.

A MINSTREL BOOK and colophon are registered trademarks of Simon & Schuster Inc.

Cover photo courtesy of Columbia Pictures Television, Inc.

Printed in the U.S.A.

The Best Things in
Life Are Free. Right?

chapter one

"Claudia! Let's get out of here," Jody Lynch called. "I want to get to the mall."

I smiled at my best friend. "Me, too." The last bell had just rung—and I couldn't wait to leave school. "Let me get my books first," I told Jody.

She followed me down the hall to my locker.

I spun the lock and yanked open the metal door. About two thousand books were crammed inside. And I needed most of them to do my homework tonight.

I glanced at Jody. She had a nearly empty black backpack slung over one shoulder. She *never* brings home books. I don't think she's ever done homework at *home* in her entire life.

I don't know how she does it. Junior high homework

is no joke. I can barely finish two math problems during study hall.

With a sigh, I began stuffing books into my pack.

Jody was staring at me. "What's with *you* today?" she asked. "You look totally bummed."

I shrugged. "I'm worried about this social studies project I have to do."

Jody frowned. "Worried—about school? Why bother?"

Jody hates school. But she's much smarter than she pretends to be. Lots of people (especially teachers) think that she doesn't understand what they're talking about. But that's not true. She just doesn't like to *seem* interested in school. She says it's not cool to like learning.

Sometimes I'm amazed that Jody and I are best friends. We're so different. Jody gets sort of rowdy sometimes. She likes to write stuff on the bathroom walls and cut school. Plus, she's totally boy crazy.

I mean, I like boys and all. But I spend more time playing my violin than chasing cute guys at the mall. Jody says I'll grow out of that.

"So why are you worried about social studies?" she asked.

I slammed my locker shut and we started down the hall. All around us, kids were pushing and shoving past, heading for the buses.

2

"It's this project for Mr. Chandler," I explained. "We have to make something that tells about our family history. It can be a video, a poster, or a diorama."

I glanced at Jody. Her head was turned so far over her shoulder, it looked as though her neck was going to break.

"There goes Todd Jackson," she said. "What a babe!"

I shook my head. "Hell*ooo!* Did you hear anything I said?"

"Sure," Jody answered. "Family history project. Chandler gave us the same assignment in first period this morning. What's the big deal? It beats fifty pages of reading a night."

"I guess. But my family history is so . . . sad," I said. "I don't know how to tell it without sounding all depressed."

"I see your point," Jody said.

Jody wasn't around when it happened, but she knows the story. A little over two years ago both my parents were killed in a car accident. I was only ten and a half. And my brother Owen was just a baby. Sometimes I worry that I'll forget what my mom and dad were like. And then I realize that poor Owen will never even *know* them.

After the accident my oldest brother, Charlie, was appointed our legal guardian. That means he's responsible for the rest of us—me, Owen, my sister, Julia, and my other brother, Bailey.

Charlie is twenty-five, so I guess Social Services thinks he's old enough to take care of us. But Charlie is always a little bit worried. If he messes up, the social workers could split us up and send us to foster homes.

But we're doing okay. That's why I really don't want to think about the sad times. Or remind anyone in school about them. For *months* after the accident everyone treated me really weird.

"And it's not just that *I* would feel sad," I told Jody. "But I don't want to tell everyone in my social studies class about my parents. I mean, the kids at my elementary school acted so sorry for me when it happened. They were all afraid to even *talk* to me."

Jody frowned. "Why?"

I shrugged. "I guess they didn't know what to say. But it was like, 'poor Claudia Salinger—she's an orphan now.' I don't want people to treat me like *that* again."

"I know what you mean," Jody said. "My friends didn't know what to say when my parents got divorced, either." She thought for a moment. "Well, maybe you should talk about your family history *before* your parents died. Or talk about when your mom and dad were kids."

I shook my head. "I wouldn't even know where to

4

start. We don't have any close relatives. I mean, who else would know our family history? I doubt if Julia, Bailey, or Charlie knows much."

Jody pushed open the glass door of the school, and we walked out into the sunlight. "You know what?" she said. "Don't worry about it, Claud. It's just a dumb project—Mr. Chandler isn't going to check if you're telling the truth. There's you, Charlie, Bailey, Julia, and Owen. The rest of the family you can make up."

"Well," I said, giving it some thought. "I could write about that gangster who was married to my aunt Phoebe."

Jody's eyes grew big. "Really?"

"Yeah," I said. "Uncle . . . Wolfgang! He used to smuggle weapons."

"Wow! Really?"

I burst out laughing. "Got you!"

"Good one." Jody smiled.

We climbed onto our school bus, number 401. I waved to my friend Jeff Bloch as I followed Jody all the way to the back. I automatically gave Jody the window seat so she could check out the boys walking past.

Jody sat down and stuck her head out the window. "Yo! Conrad!" she yelled. I knew she meant Conrad Douglas. He was suspended twice this year for fighting.

Jody plopped back down on the seat and sighed. "He is the *best* kisser."

I blinked. "He is? How do you know? Did you kiss him?" Jody is so, like, advanced compared to me.

Jody leaned over. "It was on the playground," she whispered. "In first grade."

I rolled my eyes. "Very funny."

"I'm serious," Jody said, laughing. "I told him I'd let him have my turn on the swings if he kissed me." She stared at him out the window. "I bet he's improved."

"On the swings?"

"Yeah, right."

The bus pulled away from the curb. "I can't wait to get to the mall," Jody said.

I wish I had known what she planned to do there. I probably never would have gone.

We went into the mall through Lamm's Department Store. Which was fine with me—Lamm's is the coolest. I wish I could afford to buy something there. Anything.

We walked in to the middle of the leather department, so we checked out some bags. Jody pulled a nice backpack off the rack and stuck it on my shoulder. "What do you think?"

I stared at myself in the mirror on the wall. "Nice. But I already have a backpack."

We kept walking toward the front of the store. Jody grabbed a couple of chiffon scarves. "How about these?" she asked.

"Not my style," I said.

In the juniors section Jody pulled a tight red top off the rack and held it up. "What do you think?"

"For you?" I asked.

"No, dummy. For you!"

"Dream on, Jody. I couldn't fill that out if I tried." I was barely beyond training bras.

Jody held the top up against herself and glanced into the mirror. "Cool," she said, then shoved it back into the rack. "Let's look at jewelry."

We walked over to the jewelry cases. Lamm's jewelry is the best. Whenever someone asks me what I want for a birthday or Christmas present, I tell them to get me something at Lamm's.

They have the greatest earrings. And not that expensive, either. I had my ears pierced only about a year ago, so I've been trying to collect as many pairs as I can.

Jody had her ears pierced when she was a baby. Now she's got three holes in each ear. She likes to wear a different earring in each hole.

We leaned over the jewelry counter. One of the spinning racks had all kinds of sterling-silver animal earrings.

"Look at this little pig! Isn't it cute?" I asked Jody.

"Sort of," Jody said. I could tell she didn't like the pig earrings. I put them down.

We admired some bracelets and a hair clip. On the far

side of the accessories counter was another earring rack.

Right away I spotted a pair of tiny music note earrings. Each earring was one silver note.

"Jody! Look! Aren't these great?"

I pulled the little packet off the earring carousel. We both leaned in to study them.

"Wow," Jody said. "They're you, Claud. Music notes for the fiddle girl."

Fiddle Girl. That's been Jody's nickname for me ever since we met. She thinks I spend too much time practicing my violin. But it's not a mean nickname. I know Jody thinks I'm really talented.

I flipped the earrings over to check out the price. "Whoa! Eighteen dollars. Not in my budget." I stuck them back on the spindle. "Too bad."

Jody didn't say anything.

We continued checking things out until we'd covered the whole store. "Want to go to Mason's?" I asked. "We can stop on the way at Sweet Ashley's for ice-cream cones."

Jody wrinkled her nose. "Why?"

"I don't know," I said. "I always want ice cream when I'm worried."

Jody frowned. "Worried? About that dumb family history project?"

"Sort of," I admitted.

Jody stared at me for a moment. "Ice cream sounds good," she said.

I smiled. "Let's go."

On our way out of the store, Jody suddenly stopped and turned around. "I'll catch up with you in a minute, okay?" she said. She headed back into Lamm's.

"Why?"

"I forgot something," she called over her shoulder. "I'll meet you at Sweet Ashley's."

Weird, I thought. I wonder what she forgot? I headed slowly down the mall. What kind of ice cream should I have? Chocolate double-dip? Or just plain strawberry?

"Claud!" Jody came running up behind me. "Close your eyes and open your hands," she said.

"What for?" I asked.

"Just shut up and do it," Jody ordered. She placed something small and light into my hands.

"For you. Open your eyes."

I stared down at the package in my hand. It was the little music note earrings from Lamm's.

"Jody!" I gasped. "I don't believe it!"

"Well, I wanted to cheer you up," Jody said. "Even if you don't have lots of family, you still have a best friend."

A best-friend present! This was so great.

"But, Jody, they were expensive. I can't believe you bought them for me."

I gazed down again at the two tiny earrings in my hand. They were beautiful.

Jody laughed. "Bought them? What makes you think I had the money to buy them?"

I stared at her in surprise. "But . . . but how did you get them, then?"

"Duh, Claud. I didn't *buy* them. I *stole* them."

chapter two

"Jody," I whispered. "You *stole* the earrings?"

Jody nodded. A big grin spread across her face. "Aren't they the best?" she asked.

I didn't know what to say. "I can't believe you just— you just . . . took them!"

"Yeah—I took them for you," Jody said. "Here. Put them on." She grabbed the package and pulled off one of the earrings.

"Jody, I—uh—" I stammered, moving away from her. How could I put on *stolen* earrings? I mean, what if some security guard saw her, or some hidden camera taped her or something? And the guards rushed out right now to arrest Jody—just as I was putting the earrings on?

We'd both get into huge trouble.

"I don't want to put them on right here," I said.

Jody frowned. "Why not?" she asked.

I swallowed hard. What was I supposed to do? Jody gave me these earrings to make me feel better. But now I felt awful! I didn't want to end up in trouble. I didn't want to get caught.

Jody looked annoyed. "Listen, Claud," she said. "If you don't want them, I'll take them back right now."

"No!" I cried. "You can't go back in there! You could get caught."

"Well, then, put them on," Jody said. "Don't worry. Nobody saw me take them."

"Are you sure?" I glanced around nervously. A mall security person stood guard about thirty feet away. My heart started to pound.

Jody rolled her eyes. "Yes, Claud. I'm sure."

I glanced behind me again. The security guard was busy talking to some girl. He wasn't paying any attention to us at all.

I carefully put the music notes in my ears.

Jody smiled. "Cool," she said. "Perfect for my best friend, the fiddle girl."

"Want to come over and watch TV?" Jody asked on the city bus home.

"No, thanks," I told her. "I want to get started on that social studies project."

"Already?" Jody cried. "Claud, you have, like, *ages* to do that project. It's only Tuesday!"

I thought about it. The project was due next Monday. Jody was right—I had plenty of time. But I had no idea of where to start. How was I supposed to figure out my family history without Mom and Dad here to tell it to me?

"Still, I'd rather start tonight," I told Jody. "It might take a while."

She shook her head. "Nerd," she commented. But she smiled at me. "See you tomorrow."

I waved at her as the bus pulled away from her stop.

My stop came five minutes later. While I walked home, I played with one of my new earrings—turning it around and around in my ear. The earrings were great. They were the nicest jewelry I had.

But I still felt weird. I mean, my nicest jewelry was *stolen.*

I lugged my heavy backpack up the steps to our house. San Francisco is filled with gigantic hills— which means lots of climbing up to houses on top of those hills!

When I pushed open the front door, I found Bailey and Julia standing at the foot of the stairs. Arguing. Again. They're always yelling about something.

I don't know why Bailey ever moved out of our house. He's still here all the time. To do laundry. To have dinner. To watch TV.

And to fight with Julia. Maybe he just wants to make sure it still feels like home.

Julia was wearing one of Bailey's old sweaters. That must be why he looked so mad—he hates when she borrows his things. Just like *she* hates when *I* borrow her things.

"Jules, you have it all wrong," Bailey was saying. "This isn't something extra. It's something I *need*. Why can't you understand that?"

Julia looked at Bailey like he had just landed from Mars. She's good at that. "Bay, since when is a new football something you *need?*" she cried.

I cleared my throat. They didn't turn around.

Bailey moved his face closer to Julia's. "This is not just a football, Julia. It's a limited edition Emmitt Smith football. And I *promised* the guys I would get it for the intervarsity football team at college. It's essential."

I edged closer to the front stairs. They didn't notice me.

"Oh, please." Julia rolled her eyes. "Toothpaste, that's essential. Soap, toilet paper, diapers for Owen. But we're not spending our money for the house on an overpriced football."

"Hi, guys, I'm home," I said.

Julia didn't answer. She was too busy glaring at Bailey.

"Hey, Claud," Bailey said, barely glancing in my direction. I could tell he was getting ready to yell back at Julia.

"Uh, sorry to break this up," I put in quickly. "But do either of you know where I could find out something about our family history?"

They both looked at me in surprise.

"Huh? Why?" Julia asked.

"It's for social studies. We have to find out about our ancestors and stuff."

They both kept staring at me.

"Well, do we have any old pictures or anything of our family?" I asked.

"Sure," Bailey said. "There's a box somewhere . . ." He thought for a minute. "I think it's in the attic."

"No. I moved it out of there when I moved in," Julia interrupted. Her room is so cool—it used to be the attic. But when we finally gave away Mom and Dad's old stuff, we turned it into a bedroom.

Bailey turned to me. "Actually, Claud, I think I might have seen that box in the basement. Try looking next to the dryer."

I threw my backpack on the floor and started toward the kitchen. "Thanks, guys. You can finish arguing now."

Before I even left the room, they were yelling at each other.

Our basement is really dark. Sometimes I played down there when I was little. I pretended it was a haunted cave full of creepy spirits. But really it's full of dirty laundry and boxes.

I found the box Bailey told me about right away. I pulled it off a shelf and squinted at the sagging cardboard. On the side someone had written FAMILY MEMENTOS.

Mom. Mom's handwriting. A lump rose in my throat. I could imagine her stacking everything in the box, labeling it so she would always know where to find our memories.

And now she would never see these pictures again.

But then I realized something. Maybe I didn't need anyone to tell me our family history. Mom had put it all in a box for us.

The top of the box was covered with a thick layer of dust. I brushed it off with the back of my hand. Then I pulled off the top.

Six photo albums were neatly stacked side by side. I pulled out the big white one on the end. The words OUR WEDDING were stamped in gold on the cover.

Mom and Dad's wedding album!

I flipped it open. On the first page I found their wedding invitation. And then a beautiful picture of

Mom in her wedding gown. Mom's hair was really long, and parted down the middle. She wore a crown of wildflowers in her hair. Her dress was very simple—Mom didn't go for lacy, frilly stuff. I remember that about her.

Mom wore a beautiful, happy smile on her face. It made me sad to think I would never see her smile again.

I thumbed through the rest of the album. There were more pictures of Mom and Dad and a lot of people I barely recognized. Maybe Charlie or Julia or Bailey would know who they were.

Stuck into the very back of the album I found a picture of our whole family that had been taken much later. It was Mother's Day, and we'd taken Mom on a surprise picnic to Stinson Beach. I was only in first grade then, but I still remember how much fun we had.

I set Mom and Dad's album aside and picked up the next album in the box. It had a little bunny on the cover—and under the bunny it had been stamped CHARLES SALINGER.

I couldn't believe it! Charlie's baby book! I opened it up and found his hospital infant photo. He looked like a troll.

I leaned into the box and glanced through the other albums. We were all there: Bailey, Julia, me, and Owen. Each of us had our own little book.

Perfect! I thought. I don't know why I was so worried

about my social studies project. All I have to do is look in these books—all our family memories are right here.

I went back to Charlie's book to see if there was anything about our ancestors. One of the first pages was a family tree. Yes! Mom had filled it all out.

I studied the little branches. My heart sank.

Who *were* all these people? I had never met any of them. I had never even heard of most of them. Mom and Dad didn't have any brothers or sisters, so we don't have aunts and uncles. Or cousins. These were all older relatives, people I didn't know anything about.

People I couldn't do a project about.

Just see if there are any stories about these people written in Charlie's book, I told myself. I flipped through the rest of the pages. Mom had filled out everything in the whole book. She even wrote down who came to Charlie's sixth birthday party and what kind of cake they had—chocolate with a pirate on top.

"Claudia?" Charlie yelled from the kitchen. "Dinner!"

I closed the baby book and rushed upstairs. I was starving! Charlie must have brought something home from Salinger's. That's the restaurant my dad used to own. Charlie manages it now.

"What are we eating?" I asked.

Charlie handed me five plates. "Chicken marsala. Set the table."

I started laying the plates on the kitchen table. Thurber, our bulldog, followed me. I guess he thought if I had plates, I might have food for him.

"What did you do today?" Charlie asked me.

"Went to the mall," I said.

"Did you get anything?" he asked.

I froze. The earrings! The ones Jody stole for me! Could I tell Charlie about them?

No way. He already thinks Jody is a bad influence on me.

"Not really," I said. "Um . . . I'll call Julia and Bailey." I rushed out of the kitchen, my heart pounding.

What if Charlie noticed I had new earrings? Would he ask where I got the money to buy them?

Quickly I took the earrings out.

Calm down, I told myself. Charlie has never noticed a pair of earrings in his life. Besides, it was no big deal that Jody took them.

I mean, she only stole this one time. Right?

chapter three

"Hurry up in there, Claudia!" Julia yelled the next morning. "I'm already late!"

"One more minute," I called back. I kept staring at myself in the bathroom mirror. I had a music note earring in one ear, and no earring in the other.

Should I wear the earrings to school? I couldn't decide. I mean, I really, really loved them. And they looked perfect with the London Philharmonic T-shirt I had on. And Jody would be really happy to see me wearing her best-friend present.

But the earrings made me feel so weird. Ever since last night, all I could think about when I looked at them was that Jody had *stolen* them. Would everybody be able to tell that they were stolen? I mean, they were expensive earrings. And I never wear expensive stuff.

They just made me too nervous.

"Come on, Claud! I have to get in the shower," Julia called.

I took out the earring and stared at myself some more. Would Jody be mad at me for not wearing them?

"I just won't wear any earrings," I whispered. That way, if Jody asked where they were, I could pretend I forgot to put them in. I stuffed them into the pocket of my jeans and opened the bathroom door.

"It's about time," Julia muttered.

I ignored her. I was running late now, too. I grabbed a granola bar on my way out and ran all the way to the bus stop. The bus was already waiting.

I climbed on board and glanced around for Jody. She wasn't there. She probably overslept again. Charlie makes me go to bed by ten-thirty, but Jody's mom lets her stay up as late as she wants. Sometimes that means *really* late if Jody's watching a good movie on TV. That's why she oversleeps.

When we got to school, I fought my way to my locker. Junior high is so much more crowded than elementary school. And it seems like everyone is always hurrying.

"Claud!" Jody called. She was leaning against my locker door. And Kelly Dutton stood next to her.

I was surprised to see Kelly. She and Jody have known each other since kindergarten. Kelly used to be Jody's best friend. But at the beginning of seventh grade Kelly started going out with a ninth grader named Wiley. She stopped calling Jody and started hanging out with mostly ninth graders. After a while Jody hardly ever saw Kelly.

Jody's feelings were really hurt. She and Kelly had been best friends for, like, a really long time.

That's when I came into the picture.

"How'd you get here?" I asked Jody. "You weren't on the bus."

"We got a ride with Kelly's neighbor," she answered.

"Cool," I said. I turned to Kelly. "Haven't seen you in a while."

"Wiley and I broke up," Kelly explained.

"You did?" Wow. I thought they'd be together forever. They seemed so perfect. They never fought or anything.

"I hate him," Kelly said. "He's a big jerk."

"He's going out with Tara Brice now," Jody told me.

"Ohhh. Sorry, Kelly." Tara was another ninth grader. All I knew about her was that she was head cheerleader.

Kelly sniffed. "His loss."

I nodded. But I wasn't sure what to think. Was Kelly trying to be friends with Jody again, now that her boyfriend had dumped her? I wasn't sure I liked that. Jody was *my* best friend now.

"Hey!" Jody exclaimed. "Where are your new earrings? Kelly wants to see them."

"Um . . ." I reached for my ears. "I must have forgotten to put them in."

I felt my cheeks turning red. I couldn't believe I was lying to my best friend. Quickly I dug into my pocket and pulled out the earrings. I put them in my ears.

Kelly leaned in to study them. "Cool," she said. She turned to Jody. "Were they easy to lift?"

"Piece of cake," Jody answered. She and Kelly grinned at each other.

"Kelly is the best shoplifter," Jody told me. "She's the one who taught me how to do it."

"I am not the best!" Kelly laughed. "You're just as good as I am—and you've only been doing it for a week!"

"You should have seen the first time I shoplifted, Claud," Jody said. "We were in the drugstore and there was this really stupid guy behind the counter. You know what Kelly did to distract him? She stood near the door and shouted, 'Look! It's Madonna.'"

Kelly cracked up. "He ran to the door so fast I thought his pants were on fire."

I guess I was supposed to laugh, too. But I was kind of surprised. Kelly liked to steal things, too?

Was I totally out of it? Had Jody and Kelly been hanging out again for weeks? When did Kelly teach her how to shoplift?

Jody pulled a lipstick out of her pocket.

"See? This was the first thing I took." She pulled the cap off and swiveled up the lipstick. "Carnival Melon. Kelly has the same color."

"Uh, cool." I didn't know what else to say. Jody shouldn't be stealing things—I mean, what if she got caught?

I leaned past Jody and spun the combination to my locker. Should I say something about her shoplifting? I felt funny with Kelly standing there. She would probably laugh at me.

Brrrrinng!

The five-minute bell rang. I grabbed my books off my locker shelf and slammed the door shut. "Gotta go," I said.

But when I turned around, Jody and Kelly were already ten feet down the hallway.

"Bye," I called.

"Later, Claud!" Jody answered.

She and Kelly followed Todd Jackson down the hall. I could see them with their heads bent together, whispering and laughing.

"Hi, Claudia!" I turned to see Teri Packard standing next to me. She's in my first period social studies class.

"Hey," I mumbled.

"Did you start your family history project yet?" she asked as we headed for class. "I'm almost halfway done—my dad is really into genealogy. You know, family trees and stuff."

I shrugged. "I don't know exactly what to do yet."

Teri began explaining the diorama she was planning. It was hard to listen. I mean, I really like Teri and all. But I couldn't stop thinking about Jody.

And Kelly.

She and Jody liked to do a lot of the same things. They'd been friends a lot longer than Jody and I.

What was going to happen with Jody and me? Was I about to lose my best friend?

"Hello?" I yelled when I got home. "Anyone here?"

"In the kitchen," Julia called back.

I dumped my backpack on the living room couch and headed into the kitchen. Julia sat at the table with piles of books spread all over. She glanced up when I walked into the room. "I hate term papers," she said.

"Tell me about it," I answered.

She made a face. "What do you know about term papers?"

Julia likes to think she's the only person who has schoolwork in this house.

"We did a term paper this year," I told her. "Mine was on the San Francisco earthquake—the big one that happened almost 100 years ago. We had to do references and everything."

Julia sniffed. "It's not the same," she said. "You'll see."

I love Julia, but she can be a real pain. All she ever thinks about is *her* problems.

"Fine." I sighed. "I'll be in the basement, working on *my* project."

Downstairs, I turned an empty laundry basket upside down to use as a stool. Then I pulled out the baby albums.

I looked at mine first.

Page one showed my hospital picture. I looked like a rat or something. Tons of hair sticking straight up and this weird little mouth all puckered up like I was about to cry.

There was also a picture of Mom holding me in her arms. "Ten minutes old," the caption said.

I stared at the picture for a long time. I can hardly remember what it felt like to have Mom's arms around me.

I imagined her putting these pictures in the book, thinking up the captions. Maybe she asked Dad's opinion once in a while—*"How about this, honey?"* I wished she were still here so we could go through my book together.

I turned the page and read about my first birthday. I had a party in Salinger's. I already knew how to say "Bay" and "Dada." There was a picture of Charlie holding a puppy. I leaned closer to have a better look. Whoa, it was Thurber! He was so tiny!

I slowly moved on through my twos, my threes. And then the captions began to get shorter.

After my fourth birthday, the words changed to a trickle. For my fifth birthday there was one sentence: "We went for a movie and pizza."

I flipped back and forth a couple of times. Nothing more. What happened to the rest of my memories?

I checked Bailey's book. His went through six years, just like Charlie's. So did Julia's. What had happened to *my* book?

I pulled Owen's book out. It still had plastic wrapping around it, and it looked a lot newer and cleaner than the rest of the albums. When I opened the cover, a packet of papers fell to the floor.

I picked them up and glanced through. A birth certificate, a couple of congratulation cards, and a picture of Owen and Mom in the hospital with the rest of us standing around their bed.

I skimmed the pages of Owen's album. Completely

blank. Nothing pasted in. Nothing had even been written.

"That's *it?*" I said. I stared down at the packet of papers in my hand. "That's all there is for Owen?"

It wasn't fair! He had even less than I did!

Why was Owen's book blank? I tried to remember when he was a baby. Wait! Mom and Dad died when he was only three months old!

No wonder no one had done anything with his baby book. He'd been completely left out. The rest of us had baby books. But not Owen.

It's not fair, I thought again. I don't have all my memories written down. But at least I remember Mom and Dad. Owen will never even know his parents.

And now he'll never know anything about his first few years of life, either. He'll have even fewer memories than I do.

We have to do something! I thought.

I rushed upstairs with Owen's book under my arm. I pushed open the door at the top of the stairs—and crashed right into Julia. She held the cordless phone in her hand.

"Oops," I said. "Sorry. We have to—"

"It's Jody," Julia interrupted. She handed me the phone.

Julia frowned as she stared at me. "Claud, Jody told

28

me about the earrings she gave you yesterday. I can't believe you didn't tell me about them."

I gasped. She *told* Julia? How could she do that? How could she just tell my sister I was wearing stolen jewelry?

I was going to be grounded for the rest of my life!

chapter four

Julia leaned in close to me. She stared at my earrings.
I held my breath, waiting for her to explode.

"They're really nice," she said. "I wish *I* had a friend
who'd buy me presents like that for no reason."

Buy her presents? *Buy?* I took a deep breath. Jody
hadn't told her, after all.

Julia handed me the phone and disappeared into the
living room.

"Hello?" I said.

"What's up?" Jody asked.

"Nothing. I'm going through everybody's baby albums."

"Why?"

I laughed. "Duh, Jody. We have a social studies project due Monday. Remember?"

"Oh, that," Jody said. "I haven't even thought about that. Don't tell me you *like* this family stuff."

"Well, yeah. I kind of do, now that I've started on it. Seeing pictures of my parents brings back good memories."

"I don't think I've ever even seen a picture of my parents together," Jody said. She sounded a little sad. I didn't know what to say.

"What are you doing tomorrow after school?" Jody asked quickly. She always changes the subject fast when she gets upset.

I thought about it. "I need to practice my violin. I haven't practiced once this week."

Suddenly Julia came tearing into the kitchen. "We've got to go!" she mouthed. She was helping Owen put his jacket on.

"Hold on a sec," I said into the phone. I put my hand over the receiver. "What is it?"

"We have to get to the restaurant!" Julia cried. "We're late!" She scooped up Owen and headed for the door.

"Oh, no! We forgot!" I put the receiver to my ear again. "Jody, I'll talk to you tomorrow. Bye." I quickly hung up.

Ever since Mom and Dad died, there's something the five of us do at least once every week: We meet at Salinger's for family dinner. Sometimes it's the only time we have together—the only thing that keeps us from drifting apart. No matter what, we eat together and figure out our chores for the week. Family dinner is also when we try to solve everyone's problems.

Maybe tonight I could solve Owen's baby book problem.

I grabbed his book. Then I rushed out to the driveway and climbed into the car. Owen sat in his car seat in the back. "Hi, O," I said. His mouth was covered with something sticky. "How was day care today?"

"School!" Owen yelled. For some reason, he doesn't want us to call it day care anymore. He likes to think he's a big boy.

"Sorry. How was school?"

"Jacob's party!"

I looked at Julia. She shrugged. I guess she had no idea what Owen meant, either. All he likes to talk about lately is birthday parties.

We arrived at the restaurant and hurried inside. Bailey was sitting all by himself at our usual booth.

"Where's Charlie?" I asked, sliding in next to him.

"In the kitchen," Bailey said. "Some lady wasn't happy with her steak, so he took it back." He grabbed

Owen's hand as Julia lifted him into a booster seat next to her.

Julia sat down with a dramatic sigh.

"What's with you?" Bailey asked.

"Oh, it's this stupid term paper," she complained. "I'm never going to finish it."

"That bad, huh?" Bailey said. "What's the topic?"

"Walt Whitman."

Bailey nodded seriously. "Oh. Walt Whitman."

"He's a poet, Bay," she teased him.

Bailey stuck his tongue out at her. "No kidding," he said. "I went to Walt Whitman Junior High, too."

"Please don't say those words here," I put in. "I want to forget about junior high tonight."

"Wait until you get to high school," Julia joked.

"Wait until you get to *college!*" Bailey added.

"There you are!" Charlie appeared at the table. He dropped onto the seat next to Owen. "How come you guys were so late?"

"Sorry," I said. "We weren't watching the clock."

Our waitress, Diane, showed up. I ordered my favorite, a bacon Swiss cheeseburger with double fries.

"That burger looks good, Claud," Bailey said as soon as Diane set it in front of me. He swiped a couple of my fries.

I swiped them back. "Hey! Order your own!"

Bailey grinned and dug into the huge bowl of pasta in

front of him. For a moment everyone was too busy eating to talk. It was the perfect time to bring up Owen's baby book.

"You know, guys . . ." I began.

"Charlie," Bailey cut in. "I was wondering if I could get some money. See, there's this football—"

"Oh, wait till you hear this, Charlie," Julia interrupted.

I sighed. I guess Owen's baby book would have to wait.

"I need a new football. I told the guys on my intravarsity team I would buy this special ball," Bailey explained.

Julia put her fork down. "Hold on, Bay. You do not *need* a new football. You *want* a new football."

"No," Bailey answered firmly. "Weren't you listening? I promised the guys I would buy the ball—"

"Yeah, but you don't have to buy the most expensive football in history," Julia argued. "It's not like we have an extra hundred dollars lying around in some football fund!"

"I know it's a lot," Bailey agreed. "But the whole team is counting on me. The Emmitt Smith ball will bring us good luck."

Bailey didn't have a chance. I don't know why he was even arguing. Ever since Mom and Dad died, money has been tight. I mean, Charlie makes enough managing the restaurant. And we get some money each month from the trust fund our parents left.

But still, it's not much. Not for five people.

"Julia!" Bailey finally exploded. "This isn't up to you! It's up to Charlie!"

Everyone turned to look at Charlie.

He shifted around uncomfortably in his seat. He hates to be put on the spot. But since he's our legal guardian, he has to make the final decisions.

Charlie moved his steak around on his plate. He took a sip or two of water. "I know it's important to you, Bay." He cleared his throat.

"But?" Bailey said.

Charlie frowned. "Well, money is tight this month. Remember the pipe that burst in the upstairs bathroom? That plumber's bill ate up whatever house money was left over." He fiddled with his napkin. "I'm really sorry, Bailey."

Bailey stared down at his plate. "I understand. I just thought if there was any extra . . ."

"Sorry, Bay," Charlie repeated. "Not this month."

Right then, if I could have done anything for Bailey, I would. He looked so disappointed!

No one said anything.

Well, this is awful, I thought. Family night was

supposed to be fun! Suddenly I remembered Owen's baby book. "Hey—look what I found in the basement," I said.

I set the book on the table and opened it to the first page.

Julia smiled. "Owen's book! I remember when Mom bought that."

"You do?" I asked.

"Sure," Julia said. "What's in it?"

I held up the packet of papers. "Just these cards and a picture of us and Owen. I guess she didn't have time to paste anything in before . . . you know."

"Let's see the picture, Claud," Bailey said softly.

I handed it over. Bailey's face broke into a grin. "Look how little he was!" He showed the picture to Owen. "Do you know who this is?"

Owen shook his head.

"It's you! You were only a few minutes old!"

Owen started laughing as if that were the funniest thing he'd ever heard.

"Let me see," Julia said. She leaned over to look at the photo. "You were so tiny, Owen."

"Now I big," Owen said.

Julia laughed. "Huge!" She studied the picture. "All of us are big now. Look how much we've changed." She pointed to Bailey's picture. "Nice hair, Bay."

Bailey snatched the picture back out of Julia's hand

and examined his messy hair. "Hey!" he protested. "What do you expect? It was the middle of the night!"

I snatched the picture away. Everybody looked at me. "We each have our own baby book," I announced. "They're all down in the basement."

"I know," Charlie said. "I remember Mom pasting things into them."

"Really?" Julia asked. "I don't remember that."

"Yeah. When I was little I liked to go through them and read about everyone—I even drew pictures in Bailey's. I can't believe you dug them up again, Claud."

Bailey was reading Owen's congratulation cards. "Oh, wow," he said. "This one is from the Finches. Remember the Finches? They lived two houses down. They moved to Hawaii way before O was born. I never knew Mom and Dad stayed in touch with them."

"I remember the Finches," Julia said. "They had that weird little dog. It was like a chihuahua mixed with . . . something else."

"Poodle!" Bailey cried.

"Yeah, poodle." Charlie laughed. "I'd forgotten all about them. I hated that dog!"

"Me, too," Julia said. "Remember how it always used to bark at Thurber when he was a puppy?"

"I haven't thought about the Finches in years," Bailey commented. "It's weird how we can just forget people like that."

"Well, you know what?" I put in. "I don't remember any of this. I don't even remember who the Finches were. I don't remember *anything* about when I was little."

My brothers and sister stared at me in surprise.

"Why not?" Julia asked.

"I don't know why not," I said. "Maybe because I don't have Mom and Dad here to tell me stories about when I was a baby."

"So?" Bailey asked. "What's the big deal? Nobody remembers when they were little."

"I don't," Charlie agreed.

"Yeah, but the only time I had with Mom and Dad was when I was little," I pointed out. "You guys all had a lot more time with them. You all have a lot more memories."

No one said anything.

"The only things I know about myself are the things Mom wrote in my baby book," I explained. "And Owen won't even have that. His baby book is totally blank. All it has is these cards and a baby picture."

I glanced around at my brothers and sister. "We have to do something."

"Like what?" Julia asked.

"Like start his book," I said. "It won't take that long. I just need you guys to tell me all the things that have to be filled in, like how old Owen was when he first sat up and stuff like that."

"Sophomore year," Bailey said.

"Huh?"

"It was during my sophomore year in high school. I was playing with him on the floor and I propped him up against Mr. Bear and he stayed. Remember?"

"I do," Charlie said. "I was trying to sleep, and you started screaming. I thought somebody had broken into the house."

Everyone smiled. Owen was playing with his blank book. He looked bored.

"I don't know, Claud," Julia said. "The baby books were Mom's thing. It wouldn't be the same if we did them."

I glanced at Owen. How would he feel when he grew up and found out we all had baby memories except him? "I think Mom and Dad would want us to finish Owen's book," I argued. "Since they're not here to do it."

"That's the whole point—they *aren't* here," Julia answered. "It brings up too many sad memories."

"Besides, Owen doesn't really *need* a baby book," Bailey put in. "I mean, none of us ever even look at our books."

"But it's not fair!" I cried. "You guys all remember more about Mom and Dad than I do. You even have more written in your baby books than I do. And Owen won't have anything!"

"RRRrrrrr!"

I glanced at Owen. He was running a little toy truck around the rim of his plate and making truck noises. It seemed so sad that he wouldn't have anything to show him about his childhood or his family history.

"Don't worry, Claud," Bailey said. "We'll tell him about all the important stuff."

"But when?" I asked. "What if you forget, like you forgot about our old neighbors?"

Bailey shrugged. "If we forget about things, they couldn't have been very important."

"Dessert, anyone?" Diane asked, stopping by our table.

"Yes!" Julia and Charlie said together.

Everybody began talking about dessert. I guess nobody cared about family memories except me.

Maybe that's because they *have* memories, I thought. And I don't.

And Owen never will.

chapter five

"Want to watch TV at my house tonight?" Jody asked on the way to the bus Thursday afternoon. "The refrigerator's loaded. Mom went to the store yesterday."

I glanced over at Jody. Kelly walked next to her.

Big surprise, I thought glumly. Kelly had been hanging out with Jody and me for the past two days. Correction—Kelly and Jody had been hanging out. I was there, too, but I practically felt invisible. I wasn't in on their private little jokes that went all the way back to kindergarten.

"No, thanks," I said, shaking my head. "I need to do my social studies project." It wasn't that I minded going to Jody's house. It was that I was kind of sick of Kelly. I mean, was I supposed to suddenly be friends with her just because she broke up with some dumb guy?

Jody rolled her eyes. "Oh, please, Claud. Who cares about stupid family stuff? I wish I'd never heard of my relatives. Every time I go to my cousins' house, all I hear about is how good they are in school, and how many hobbies they have, blah, blah."

Kelly laughed. "You mean your cousins Johanne and Tina?"

Jody nodded. "Remember when we sabotaged Johanne's eighth birthday party?"

"Yeah—we told the magician the wrong address and he never showed up." Kelly cracked up. "That was the best!"

"But my grandmother was so mad," Jody went on. "She hates me."

"Jody!" I cried. "Don't say that. Your grandmother can't *hate* you."

Jody shrugged. "I guess not. But I can't stand her. My mom says Nana and I are really alike, so we get on each other's nerves. But I don't think I'm anything like her."

"Well, you look like her," Kelly put in.

"Yeah, yeah, and we're both left-handed and we both love art and we both have red hair," Jody said. "Mom tells me that all the time—I got my looks and everything from Nana. Big deal."

"But she's your *grandmother,*" I said. "How can you not love her—especially if she's just like you?"

Jody shrugged again. "I don't know. She's a pain."

I glanced down at my feet. Sometimes I just don't get Jody. I mean, she had a grandmother who was just like her—and she didn't care!

I was left-handed, too. I was the only one in the family. And I had no idea where I got it from. Maybe one of *my* grandmothers was left-handed. Maybe that's where it came from.

But I'll never know, I realized. My parents aren't around to tell me things like that. I'll never know who I'm like.

And neither will Owen.

Jody and Kelly were still talking about Jody's annoying cousins.

"Here's the bus, Jody," I announced. She was so busy remembering that she almost walked right by it.

"Oh. I'm going to walk home with Kelly," Jody said. "You sure you don't want to come over?"

"No, thanks," I answered.

"Okay," Jody said. "But you're going to miss a great time."

It was weird—Jody never walked home with me. We always rode the bus. It would take forever to walk all the way home. And Jody hates walking.

So how come she was walking home with Kelly?

I tried to act cheerful as I got onto the bus. But I was really worried now. Jody and Kelly were so alike. And they had known each other since they were really little.

No wonder they'd been best friends. Maybe Jody was getting sick of me. Maybe she thought I was boring because I did my homework instead of hanging out with her. Maybe she wanted to be with Kelly again.

What was I supposed to do about it?

"Anybody home?" I yelled, shutting the front door behind me.

No one answered. I usually got home first, but sometimes Bailey came over, or Charlie had to bring Owen home early from day care. You never knew who would be home in our house.

I dumped my backpack on the couch and headed straight into the kitchen. I had a snack of milk and Oreos to make myself feel better. Charlie must have done some grocery shopping because the refrigerator and freezer were stuffed.

While I ate, I studied the assignment sheet from Mr. Chandler again and tried to forget about Kelly and Jody having a great time somewhere.

"Create a multimedia project that tells us about one or more aspects of your family history. Some questions

44

you may want to include: Where do your ancestors come from? How did your family end up in San Francisco? Do you have any special family stories that have been passed down over the years about your ancestors?"

"I have no idea," I said out loud. Maybe Jody was right—I *should* make a few things up.

It was time to do some serious hunting. I went downstairs to the basement and hauled the Family Mementos box back upstairs. I could spread everything out on the kitchen table.

I was surprised to find Julia there.

"Whoa. Where did you come from?" I asked.

"I just brought Owen home," she answered. She began spreading her papers and note cards out on the table. "I have to work on my term paper." She covered the entire table with her stuff.

I was still holding the box of albums—which weighed about five hundred pounds. "But I was doing my homework here."

"You were?"

I dropped the box with a loud thud and grabbed the piece of paper with Mr. Chandler's assignment. Julia had dropped her books right on top of it.

"See? Proof!" I waved the paper in her face.

Julia frowned. "Can you find someplace else?"

"Not really. Can you move over?"

"Not really. I need to spread out."

"So do I."

Owen barged into the room grasping three crayons. "Ju-lee!" he yelled. He climbed up onto a chair beside Julia and started coloring her index cards.

"Owen! Stop!" Julia grabbed the cards away and took a couple sheets of blank paper. "Here, O. Color these instead, okay?" She sighed.

Owen scribbled away. Now there were *two* people at my table. Obviously, it was pretty pointless for me to ask for some room.

Julia glanced up. "Why don't you go work on the dining room table? I'm sure it's quiet in there." She smiled. I could tell she was trying to be nice.

"Oh, all right," I said. I dragged the box of albums into the dining room. It's always kind of dark in there, not really the greatest place to do homework. But at this point I was happy to find another big space.

I heaved the box onto the table. Okay. Now what? I guess the best place to start on a family history project would be the family tree.

I flipped to the tree in Charlie's book. But it didn't help me at all. I mean, I could just copy it down and hand it in for my social studies project. But that wouldn't really tell the story of my family's history. It wouldn't answer the questions Mr. Chandler had asked.

The names on the family tree were so weird. Margaret Craig. Edmond Farrell. Jane Mancie.

Mom's grandparents. Dad's great-uncles.

I had never heard of any of them. I didn't remember Mom or Dad ever talking about them.

With a sigh, I glanced back at the other albums. Charlie and Bailey and Julia just don't get it, I thought. They don't understand how Owen will feel when he gets older.

He'll feel exactly the way I do now. I should make his baby book myself.

"That's it!" I cried.

"What?" Julia called from the kitchen.

"What?" Owen yelled.

"It's a surprise," I called back. The perfect surprise, I added silently. A baby book—*and* a social studies project!

I would make Owen's baby book myself—and tell the story of our family while I did it. Mr. Chandler didn't say the project had to be ancient family history. It could be our family's history over the last few years.

And I wouldn't need to know all our family stories—I could just add little Owen stories like the one Bailey told about the first time Owen sat up. And I could maybe talk about what it was like before we had Owen and how things changed when he came.

As much as I could remember, anyway.

I grinned to myself. My history wouldn't have to be sad this way. It would be a story about how our family memories kept going. I mean, the family didn't *stop* after Mom and Dad died.

It just changed.

I grabbed Owen's album out of the box and opened it up. Wait till I tell Jody! I thought. Then I remembered how dumb she thought this project was. Okay. Maybe I wouldn't tell her about it. She and Kelly would probably just laugh, anyway.

The first few pages of Owen's book were easy. From his birth certificate I was able to fill in his birth date, where he was born, what time, and who was there. Under "First Visitors" I wrote "Claudia, Charlie, Bailey, and Julia." I mean, who else could it have been?

And suddenly I remembered it! The four of us clustered around Mom and Dad and this tiny baby. I remembered how weird it felt to have a little brother. I had always been the youngest—and then all of a sudden I wasn't. I didn't mind, though, because I loved Owen so much. As soon as I saw him, it was like I had always had a baby brother.

I wrote about the huge banner we had hung across the front door when Mom and Owen came home from the hospital.

Then I moved to the next page: Owen's family tree. I

copied it out of Charlie's book. I tried to remember if Mom or Dad had ever mentioned any of these people. Alonzo Phelps, Elizabeth Phelps, Henry Weir . . . Owen Weir!

Finally! *Something* about my family that I remember! Owen Weir was Mom's uncle—my great-uncle. He played the saxophone. I remember, because Mom said that if I'd been a boy, my name would have been Owen.

Across from the family tree was a little section called: "How I Got My Name." I wrote up the story of Great-uncle Owen, and how Mom admired him because he was musical like her.

The next page was called "Firsts." There were places to list dates for Owen's first smile, first step, and everything else.

"First tooth . . ." How should I know when he got his first tooth? I just guessed . . . one year old maybe? I wrote it down. No, wait. He had lots of teeth by then. After the *one* I scratched out *year* and wrote *month*.

I filled in the rest of the page the same way, putting in what I could remember.

The next page was called "My First Birthday." Now *that* I remembered clearly. We threw a big party for him in the backyard. I strung crepe paper all along the bushes. And Owen cried because he was afraid of his birthday candles.

I glanced down at the baby book. Each page had a little pouch for photographs. Where were the pictures from that party? Maybe the kitchen drawer?

I ran upstairs. Julia and Owen still sat at the table.

"Hey, Jules?" I said as I yanked open the junk drawer.

"Mmm-hmmm?" She didn't even look up from her book.

"Remember that picture of Owen at his first birthday eating his birthday cake?"

"Cake. Party!" Owen shouted.

"That's right, Owen. You were one! Jules, have you seen that picture anywhere?"

"I think it's somewhere in that drawer," Julia told me.

I shuffled through old address books, pencils, rubber bands, and shopping coupons. Where was that thing?

I looked and looked until I found it! I pulled it out and studied it. It was kind of wrinkled and bent, but it would flatten out once I pasted it in the book.

And then Owen would have his memories.

chapter six

"Where's Jody?" my friend Jeff asked as I sat down on the bus the next morning.

I shrugged. I wasn't even surprised that Jody missed the bus again. She probably stayed with Kelly last night. Kelly—her new best friend.

I opened my Spanish book and studied verbs until we got to school. I was getting used to spending time without a best friend.

When I finally got to school, Jody was waiting for me right in front of my locker. Unfortunately, so was Kelly.

"Hi, Jody. Hi, Kelly," I said. I wanted to be nice to Kelly since she was Jody's friend, but I was having a hard time. "How did you get to school?"

Jody shrugged. "I got a ride with Kelly."

"Why?" I asked. "I mean, why didn't you just take the bus like you usually do?"

"I missed it," Jody said matter-of-factly. "How else could I get here?"

"Duh, Claud," Kelly said. "Jody doesn't need any more late slips."

"*I* know that," I told her. Since when had Kelly become an authority on Jody's life, anyway? I wished she would butt out.

The five-minute bell rang. I opened my locker and put my books inside. "So . . . we better get going, right?" I wasn't sure why Kelly was still standing there. Were we all supposed to walk together to our next class like one big happy family?

Jody broke into a grin. "First, a surprise. Kelly and I got you something at the mall yesterday."

"The mall?" I repeated. "I thought you were just going to watch TV last night."

"What fun would that be?" Kelly asked.

"Really, Claud," Jody added.

I didn't know what to say. Jody and I always hang out and watch TV. We have so much fun laughing at the commercials and singing along with music videos and stuff.

At least, I *thought* we had fun. But maybe Jody didn't really like to do that. Maybe she thought it was boring.

Maybe she liked going to the mall with Kelly better than just hanging out at home with me.

"What did you do at the mall?" I asked.

"We had the best time," Kelly told me. "We met these really hot ninth graders, and they bought us pizza."

"It was incredibly cool," Jody added.

I couldn't believe it. My best friend was hanging out at the mall without me—and she didn't even care that I wasn't there.

"You should have come, Claud," Jody said. "We got some really cool stuff. Here's what I got for you."

Jody pulled a necklace out of her backpack and handed it to me. "What do you think?"

"Oh, wow!" I gasped. It was beautiful—a silver necklace with music notes on it to match my earrings.

Jody grinned. "I knew you'd like it!" She turned to Kelly. "Didn't I tell you Claudia would love this?" Jody poked my arm. "Another five-finger discount."

"Oh." Suddenly I didn't like the necklace so much. It was really pretty, but Jody had stolen it just like she stole the earrings.

"You should see Jody," Kelly told me. "I think she's better at it than I am now."

"Great," I murmured. Just great, I thought. Jody is turning into a regular kleptomaniac. Didn't she know she could get in trouble?

"Well," Jody said. "Aren't you going to put it on?" She and Kelly stared at me, waiting.

"Well . . ."

"Hey. You're not freaking out because I didn't pay for this, are you?" Jody asked.

"I think it would be nice if you paid for something once in a while," I admitted. "I mean, I really love my earrings. And the necklace. But you could, like, go to jail or something, Jody."

Jody laughed. "You're such a wimp, Claud. Why would they send me to jail? The store doesn't care if a few things disappear. They expect it. That's why they have insurance."

"It is?" I asked.

"Yeah," Kelly agreed. "Don't be a dweeb, Claudia. People shoplift all the time."

"They do?" Could that be right? Jody and Kelly seemed so positive.

The final bell rang. "Do you want that necklace or not?" Jody demanded.

"If you don't want it, I'll take it," Kelly offered.

"No!" I said quickly. No way would I let Kelly have something that Jody had picked out for me.

I still felt strange wearing something that I knew was stolen. But Jody gave the necklace to *me,* to go with her best-friend present. And if Kelly took it instead, it would seem like *she* was Jody's best friend.

"I like it. I really do. It's perfect." I held the necklace up to my neck and Jody fastened the clasp.

"Thanks, Jody," I said. "I love it."

I checked myself out in the mirror on my locker door. The necklace did look cool. And no one else would know it was stolen, I told myself.

Besides, if I didn't wear the necklace, I might lose my best friend for good.

chapter seven

"Hey, Fiddle Girl. What's up?" Jody called Friday morning.

I glanced around the bus, expecting to see her with Kelly. Instead, she was alone.

I grinned as I dropped into the backseat next to her.

"Nothing much," I said.

She reached into her pocket and held out her hand. "Hey! Check out this eye shadow I took from the drugstore last night. It goes with my lipstick. Mad Melon. Nice, huh?" She twisted open the lid and sniffed. "It even smells like melon."

I stared down at the eye shadow. Did Jody steal something, like, every day?

"Jody, you've got to stop this," I blurted out.

She glanced up at me. "Stop what?"

"Shoplifting! You keep taking things! What if you get caught?" I asked.

Jody rolled her eyes. "Are you going to start on that again? What's the big deal? Shoplifting is fun."

She shoved the eye shadow back into her pocket. "Besides, I don't see you complaining about your new earrings and that necklace."

"I didn't want those things!" I told her. "I didn't ask you to steal things for me."

Jody stared at me. "What's your problem, Claud? Why do you have to give me a hard time? Kelly doesn't act this way when I take things!"

I couldn't believe it. How could Jody even say something like that? How could she compare Kelly to me?

"Yeah, well, *Kelly* isn't really a great friend," I snapped. "She dumped you for Wiley, remember? She doesn't care if you get in trouble."

"That's not true," she said. "She *does* care. And she's a lot more fun than you lately."

The bus pulled up in front of school. Jody grabbed her bag and started angrily down the aisle. I followed her.

"Hey!" I yelled. "What's that supposed to mean? Huh? She's more fun because she shoplifts?"

Jody didn't answer. Instead, she shoved open the door to the school and headed straight to the girls' bathroom. I stormed in after her.

How could Jody say that Kelly was more fun? How could she?

The bathroom was packed with girls I didn't know. The only one I recognized was Caroline Suh. She's one of the popular girls in our class.

"Everybody move," Jody commanded. "No hogging the mirror."

No one even turned around. Then one person stepped away from the last sink. Kelly. She waved at Jody.

Oh, great, I thought. Just who I wanted to see.

Jody went over and squeezed into Kelly's spot. "Thanks, Kel," she said. She turned her back to me.

"Any time," Kelly answered.

I was sort of standing behind them, feeling stupid. What was I supposed to do? Leave? Stay? Tap Kelly on the shoulder and tell her I was there?

"Hey, Claud," Caroline called from the sink next to Jody.

"Hi," I called back.

Kelly glanced at me. "Oh, hi, Claudia," she said with a fake smile. "I didn't see you!"

Yeah, right, I thought. I must blend in really well with bathroom tile.

Jody ignored me. She handed the eye shadow to Kelly. "I picked this up last night, remember?"

Kelly grinned. "Of course I remember. It was a blast!"

"Try some," Jody told her. "It's a great color for you."

"Okay," Kelly said. She had on a ton of eye shadow already, but she quickly added the Mad Melon on top. When she was finished, she turned around. "Do you want a turn, Claudia?"

"No, she doesn't," Jody interrupted in a loud voice. "Claudia is too good to use things that are stolen."

Suddenly the girls nearby stopped talking. They all stared at me. I could feel my face turning red. Why were they staring?

Were they surprised that Jody was a shoplifter? Or did they just think I was a goody-goody because I didn't like her shoplifting?

"That's not what I meant," I told Jody. "I just don't want to get in trouble. I mean, I don't want you to get in trouble. . . ."

A girl at the sink next to Caroline began to giggle. Was she laughing at *me?* Was I the only one in the world who cared that Jody *stole* the eye shadow?

I squeezed myself behind Kelly so that I stood near the wall. None of those other girls would be able to hear me from here.

"Well, I *won't* get in trouble," Jody muttered.

"You only get in trouble if you get caught!" Caroline joked. She pushed her long dark hair over her shoulders and studied herself in the mirror.

"Jody's too good at it to get caught," Kelly put in.

"Oh, no one ever gets caught," Shannon Wilson said. She's in ninth grade. I think she's a friend of Kelly's— she was standing right behind her. "Besides, the store would just make you put back what you took."

Shannon finished brushing her hair and headed out of the bathroom.

My cheeks still felt hot. I guess I never thought about this before. Could you really just go into a store and take whatever you wanted?

"Come on, Claudia," Caroline said. "Don't tell me you've never stolen anything."

I shook my head.

"Not even a piece of candy?" Caroline asked. "Not even when you were little?"

"No," I insisted.

Caroline laughed. "Well, everybody does it sometimes," she teased me. "Everybody but *you*, I guess."

"Hey," Kelly suggested. "Maybe you'd stop being nervous if you lifted something, Claudia. Then you'll know it's no big thing."

I gasped. *Me?* Shoplift? No way!

Jody grinned. "Yeah, Claud. Come with us next time we go to the mall!"

"You're kidding, right?" I said. My voice sounded kind of squeaky.

"No," Jody answered. "Why would I be kidding?"

She couldn't mean it. She knew I couldn't steal anything.

"But I . . ." My heart started to pound. "What if I got caught?"

"You saw how easy it was for me the other day," Jody pointed out. "We'll go after school today. What do you say?"

She was serious! She was really serious! "But—but—" I didn't know what to say. There was no way I could ever take something. I'd be way too scared.

"Forget it, Jody," Kelly said. She pointed to me. "Look at her. She's petrified just thinking about it. She could never actually *do* it."

She was right! No way could I shoplift.

"Yes, she can," Jody insisted. "Right, Claudia?"

They both stared at me, waiting for an answer. I felt trapped. I wanted to show Jody I was just as much fun to hang out with as Kelly was.

But Kelly was right—I was way too chicken. How could I get out of this?

"I'm . . . not sure," I admitted.

Kelly laughed. "Told you," she said to Jody. "She's too scared."

"You guys are being mean," Caroline put in. "You can't *make* Claudia shoplift if she doesn't want to."

"You're right," Jody said. "Never mind, Claudia."

Kelly turned her back to me and started putting on more makeup in the mirror. So did Jody. I felt like a total nerd.

A nerd without a best friend.

Kelly and Jody were talking to each other like I wasn't even there. "Remember last week in Mason's?" Jody asked Kelly. "You dared me to go into the cosmetics department and take the perfume tester off the counter?"

Kelly rolled her eyes. "That was *so* funny. You just picked it up and walked right past the security guard."

"And then we tried it on," Jody finished. She held her nose. "Nasty. It totally wasn't worth taking."

They both laughed. I laughed, too. Sort of.

"Yesterday I got this great turquoise ring," Kelly said. She held out her hand to show Jody.

"Nice," Jody agreed.

The more they talked, the worse I felt. Jody was disgusted with me—I was sure of it. She wouldn't even look at me.

"I got it at Utopia," Kelly added. "I bought it. But I bet you could lift one."

"You think?" Jody said.

Kelly nodded. "That place is cool. No one is ever watching. You can take whatever you want there."

Caroline rolled her eyes. "You guys are a little too obsessed with shoplifting," she said. "I'm out of here."

They didn't even answer her as she pushed her way through the crowd to the door.

Kelly dug in her backpack. "Here. Look at this keychain I got at Utopia."

She pulled out a small plastic object. "It's a little lava lamp." She cupped her hands around the keychain, and it went from dull gray to bright orange.

Jody nodded. "That is *nice.*"

The bathroom was so crowded that we'd been pushed into a tiny corner. I felt hot. Sweaty. I wanted out of there.

Jody and Kelly had completely forgotten about me.

I was beginning to wonder if Jody would ever talk to me again.

The bell rang. "Time to go," Kelly said. She looked at Jody and they both said, "Duh!" at the same time. They laughed and started for the door.

Suddenly Jody stopped and turned to me. "Claud, we're going to the mall right after school," she said. "Are you coming?"

"We won't *make* you steal anything," Kelly added.

"Claud?" Jody prodded me.

I glanced at Kelly. She obviously didn't want me to go to the mall with them. And even if I didn't shoplift, Kelly and Jody probably would.

But if I didn't at least go to the mall with them, Jody would never want to hang out with me again.

"Sure," I said. "I'll go."

chapter eight

So," Jody said, popping a stick of gum in her mouth. "Where should we go first?"

I shrugged and stared out the window of the bus. We were almost at the mall. I couldn't stop worrying.

I mean, if Jody and Kelly were going to steal things, and I knew about it, didn't that make *me* some kind of criminal, too? If I saw them shoplifting, wasn't I supposed to make a citizen's arrest or something?

"Mason's," Kelly suggested. "I need perfume. I dumped the stuff Wiley gave me down the toilet."

"Good for you," Jody said.

"Yeah," I added, even though I didn't care.

For the rest of the way there, Jody and Kelly gossiped

about people at school. They talked a lot about Wiley and Tara, but I wasn't paying any attention.

And they weren't paying any attention to me, either.

When we got to the mall, Jody jumped out of her seat and headed for the door. "Come on, Claud!"

I stood up slowly. Why did I feel so nervous? I wasn't the one planning to steal things.

Forget it, I thought. I should just have fun.

I hopped down the bus stairs and followed Jody and Kelly toward the mall. "Hey, wait up!" I called.

Jody turned around and smiled. "We're going to start at Mason's."

"Okay—anywhere you want."

Mason's Department Store is the biggest store in the mall. It has everything you'd ever want, including groceries. We stopped in front of the entrance.

"Let's get your perfume first," Jody told Kelly. "I want some, too. Summer Melon perfume—to go with my eye shadow and lipstick."

"Cool," Kelly said. "Let's go." She led the way into the store.

My stomach turned to knots. I stared at my feet as I wandered down the main aisle of Mason's.

All the salespeople can probably take one look at us and know we're shoplifters, I thought.

"Claud!" Jody yelled.

I jumped. "What?"

"Relax," Jody said. "You almost walked into that display counter."

"Oh. Thanks."

"Your face is all red," Jody pointed out. "What's wrong with you?"

"Nothing," I said.

"Are you guys coming or not?" Kelly called. She was already twenty yards ahead of us.

I followed Jody through the scarves and bags to the cosmetics department.

"Let's just walk around for a few minutes and check things out," Kelly suggested.

"Fine," I said. "Good idea."

Kelly steered us to the JUMP counter. They have cool makeup in crazy colors like pastel blue and green. Jody and Kelly opened a few of the samples and tried on some eye shadow, lipstick, and eyeliner.

I looked around for salespeople. Or security guards. Or anyone. But nobody was watching us. I began to feel a tiny bit better.

"What do you think?" Jody asked me.

I turned to look at her. She stood in front of a big mirror, holding up a huge bottle of perfume.

"Look! It's Summer Melon," she added.

"Jody!" I yelped. "Hide it! What are you doing?"

Jody's mouth fell open. "What?" she cried. "What's wrong?" She frantically glanced around.

"Everyone can see you," I whispered, yanking her arm down. "Aren't you supposed to, like, stick it in your pocket or something?"

Jody burst out laughing. "No, dweeb. I'm not *stealing* it. I'm trying it on." She showed me the bottle. A big pink label said TESTER.

I felt my face get warm.

"Oh." I felt so stupid. "Good."

Jody was still giggling. But luckily Kelly had wandered away. She hadn't seen me act like an idiot.

Jody punched my arm. "You have to relax, okay? I'm not going to steal everything I see."

"Okay," I said. I felt embarrassed. Jody must think I'm such a baby.

"I was going to *buy* this perfume," she said. "Do you like it?" She held out her arm.

I sniffed. "It's nice," I mumbled.

"Okay. Now I'm going to get out my money and give it to the cashier," Jody said slowly. "Think you can handle that without attacking me, Fiddle Girl?"

I met Jody's eyes. She was teasing me. I couldn't help smiling back at her. "I guess I can take it," I said. "But if you try to steal one of the mannequins, I'm calling the cops."

"Deal," Jody said. We both laughed.

Jody brought the Summer Melon to a cashier and paid for it. Then we went to find Kelly.

"Okay, watch what she's doing," Jody told me when we spotted Kelly's blond hair at the back of the cosmetics department.

I stared at Kelly. "She's just walking around," I said.

"Not really," Jody whispered. "See, you have to make it look like you're just browsing. You pick something up, maybe check out the price, put it back, then move on to the next place. Get it?"

I kept watching Kelly. The whole time Jody was talking, Kelly wandered around the cosmetics counters. Sometimes she would stop and look at something. Then she would put it down and keep walking. Once or twice she glanced at a price tag.

She looked totally calm and relaxed.

Then she stopped near the cologne sprays. They were all displayed on a countertop—with no glass around them or anything.

I glanced around for the saleswoman. She was on the other side of the counter, helping a customer.

Our eyes locked. She smiled. I smiled. "I'll be with you in a minute," she called.

"No, no." I waved my hands. "I'm just looking, thanks."

Oops! I didn't mean to get someone's attention! I just wanted to make sure no one was watching Kelly!

Did I ruin everything? I wondered. Is that saleswoman going to be looking at us now?

Quickly I turned away. Act natural, I told myself. I picked up a tube of lip gloss off the counter in front of me and pretended to look at it.

Is that saleswoman still watching? I wondered. Is she going to stop Kelly from taking the perfume? I glanced up.

Kelly stood right in front of me. She must be really mad at me, I thought. I got ready to be yelled at.

"Thanks, Claud," Kelly said.

"Huh?"

"That was good," Kelly told me. "You distracted her."

"Did you get the perfume?" Jody asked.

"Yup," Kelly said. "It's right in my bag."

I gasped. "You took it? Right now? While I was talking to the saleswoman?"

Jody and Kelly grinned. "Sure," Kelly said. "She was busy looking at you, so it was the perfect time to take something!"

Wow. Even *I* didn't notice Kelly take the perfume— and I knew she was going to do it!

In fact, I sort of helped her do it.

"Are you taking that?" Kelly asked.

"What?" I glanced down at my hand. I hadn't even realized I was still holding the lip gloss. "No!"

"You should take it, Claud," Jody whispered.

I shook my head. What about that saleswoman? I glanced over at her. She had her back to me.

"Just take it," Kelly put in.

"I can't!"

"Here—" Jody pulled open her shopping bag with the Melon perfume in it. "Drop it in here!"

"No!"

"Claud! Nobody's looking," Jody insisted. "Just take it. Now! Drop it in the bag!"

I glanced at the saleswoman.

She began to turn toward me.

Quickly I dropped the lip gloss into Jody's bag.

The saleswoman smiled at me again. I didn't know what to do. I tried to smile back.

"Let's go," Jody said loudly. "I don't want to buy anything else." She slung the shopping bag over her arm and began walking toward the front of the store.

I followed her through the doors and out into the mall. Nothing happened. Nobody came by. Nobody even looked at us.

Was that it? Did this mean I didn't get caught?

Jody and Kelly led me to a bench and sat down. I collapsed beside them. "Oh, wow," I gasped. "That was *horrible.*"

"What's wrong?" Jody asked. "You did it!"

"I can't believe I stole something," I murmured.

"Wasn't it easy?" Kelly asked me.

"I guess," I said. "But still . . ."

"Wasn't it fun?" Kelly asked.

I thought about that for a minute. Now that my heart had stopped pounding, the whole thing *did* seem sort of fun.

Jody and Kelly were grinning at me.

I was still nervous, but I started giggling. Pretty soon all three of us were giggling.

"I guess it was fun," I admitted. "No one saw us."

"Claudia!" a voice yelled.

I turned around.

"Bailey!" I cried.

Bailey! At Mason's! Did he see me?

Did he know I stole the lip gloss?

chapter nine

Bailey, what are you doing here?" I asked as he pulled me aside. I tried to make my voice sound normal.

"I wanted to get a present for my girlfriend," Bailey explained. "Some perfume."

I froze. Bailey was in the cosmetics department! With me! I was doomed.

"Listen," Bailey said. "I'm supposed to watch Owen tonight. Can you do it for me?"

I let out a huge sigh of relief. Owen. He wanted to talk to me about Owen.

"Sure, Bay," I said happily. "No problem."

"Thanks, Claud," he said. "I have a big exam tomorrow. I really have to study tonight."

I nodded.

"Got to go," Bailey said. "I have ten minutes to find some perfume before I have to get to class."

"Here. Try this," Kelly said. She sprayed some of her stolen perfume in his face. "Like it?"

He took a step or two back. "Uh, yeah. It's nice."

"It's Claudia's favorite," Kelly said with a giggle.

I felt like punching her. It wasn't funny that my brother almost caught me *stealing!*

"Are you okay, Claud?" Bailey asked. "You don't look so good."

"I'm fine," I said. I smiled big. Deep breath, Claudia. Deep breath, I coached myself.

"Okay. Well, see you later," he said. "Thanks."

"Bye, Bay." We all watched him walk away.

"That was close," Jody said.

"Tell me about it," I answered.

"First word . . ." I murmured.

It was Saturday morning, and I couldn't sleep. I *always* sleep late on weekends. But I guess I was still thinking about yesterday—about shoplifting that lip gloss. And how Bailey almost caught me.

I was hoping I could take my mind off it by working on my social studies project.

But so far it was awful. I could not remember what Owen's first word was. I checked back to my first word:

Mama. But Owen has never had anyone to call Mama. That couldn't be it.

Bailey's first word was *juice.* No—that didn't ring a bell.

I stared at Owen's book. "First word . . . Claudia!" I filled in. Well, it's the first word *I* remember.

The next page was a list of Owen's favorite things. I had just filled in his favorite song when the phone rang. Who could be calling this early? I ran over and picked it up before it woke anyone. "Hello?"

"I knew you'd be awake," Jody said.

"You must be a mind reader," I told her. "I'm never up this early."

"So what's up?" she asked.

"I'm working on Owen's baby book," I answered. "I'm finishing it for him."

"That's really nice of you," Jody said. Her voice sounded a little jealous. "I wish I had a baby book."

"Maybe you do. Ask your mom."

"Are you kidding?" Jody said. "The last thing she wants to be reminded of is my baby years. That's when she and Dad got divorced. Mom had to, like, get a job and pay rent and deal with me, a tiny baby. And then I got sick and had to be hospitalized for some weird stomach thing."

"Wow," I said. "That sounds awful, Jody."

"Yeah," she answered. "I guess it was. I don't remember anything about it."

"Well, maybe you can do your report about your mom—"

"Ugh—I don't want to think about homework," Jody interrupted. "It's Saturday! So . . . do you want to do something today?"

"How about a movie?" I suggested.

"There's nothing good out," Jody answered. We both thought for a minute.

"Too bad it's raining," I said. "We could go Rollerblading in Golden Gate Park."

"Or hang out in Chinatown," Jody said.

I tried hard to think of something.

"Do you want to go to the mall?" Jody asked.

"Uh . . ." That was the last place I wanted to go. "I'm not sure, Jody."

"Listen, Claudia. I know you were nervous yesterday," Jody said. "But don't worry. We'll just shop. No lifting. I swear."

I felt a thousand times better. "Okay. Then I'll go."

"Good. Meet me at eleven at Mason's shoe department. I convinced my mom to give me money for new hiking boots."

"Cool," I said.

"Yeah, I think she's feeling guilty about neglecting me so much," Jody went on. "Ever since she got that promotion at work she's had to work late almost every night."

"Bummer," I said. "Okay. See you later." I hung up the phone and ran upstairs to get dressed.

"Hey, Claud," Charlie said, stumbling into the kitchen. "What are you doing up so early?"

"Working on my social studies project," I told him. I shoved Owen's book under a bunch of papers. I still planned to surprise everyone with his finished baby book.

"How's it going?" Charlie asked. He likes to act interested in my schoolwork. He thinks he should, since I don't have parents around to pay attention to my grades.

"It's okay, I guess," I said. "But I don't know anything about our family history. We're, like, the family with no past."

Charlie chuckled. "What do you mean?"

"Well, look at all these weird people on our family tree," I said. I pulled out his book and showed him all the names Mom had filled in.

"Like, who is Jane Mancie?" I asked.

Charlie shrugged.

"And what about this one—Alonzo Phelps?"

"He was Mom's grandfather," Charlie said. He pulled open the refrigerator and began hunting through it.

"Duh, Charlie," I said. "I can see that. But we don't know anything about him. I mean, I've never even heard of him."

"Oh, I have," Charlie told me. "I got his cuff links."

I spun around in my chair. Charlie was drinking orange juice from the carton.

"What?" I cried.

He lowered the carton and looked at me in surprise.

"What do you mean, you got his cuff links?" I said. "I've never even *heard* of my great-grandfather, and you're walking around in his cuff links?"

Charlie shrugged. "I don't wear them very often."

"How come you have Alonzo's cuff links?" I asked.

"They were my big twelfth birthday present," Charlie said. He pulled out a frying pan and began cracking eggs into it.

"What was your big present?" Julia asked. I turned to see her standing in the doorway, holding Owen on one hip.

"Grandpa Lon's cuff links," Charlie told her.

Julia smiled. "I got Great-aunt Margaret's amethyst earrings."

"Earrings?" I cried. "You have family earrings?"

78

She made a face. "They're clip-ons. They really hurt if I wear them for too long. But they're pretty."

"Bailey got the best twelfth-birthday present, though," Charlie went on. "He got Grandpa Salinger's gold money clip. He can actually *use* his present."

"Wait a minute," I said. "Are you telling me that you *all* got family gifts on your twelfth birthday?"

Julia and Charlie glanced at each other.

"Well, yeah," Charlie said. "I guess it was sort of a tradition or something. Didn't you know that?"

"No!" I cried.

"Mom told me this whole story about Great-aunt Margaret and her earrings," Julia put in. "Uncle Edmond gave them to her when they got engaged. Mom said they were really special, so I had to take good care of them. . . ." Her voice trailed off.

"Yeah, I got the same speech about the cuff links," Charlie agreed. He took Owen from Julia and sat him in his booster seat.

"Hey," Julia said. "That was probably the whole point! Like, we were twelve—so we were old enough to have nice things and be responsible for them."

Charlie laughed. "I never even thought of it that way," he said. "But it's a really good idea."

"Want breakfast, O?" Julia asked Owen.

"Beckfast!" Owen agreed.

"The eggs will be done in a minute," Charlie told them.

"Excuse me," I said loudly. Charlie and Julia looked at me. "*I'm* twelve," I announced. "In fact, I'm almost thirteen."

They just kept staring at me.

"*I* never got a family gift for my twelfth birthday!" I cried. "*I* never got a story about my relatives, or a lecture about being responsible."

"Well, Claud," Julia said. "That's because Mom and Dad weren't here for your twelfth birthday."

"No kidding!" I yelled. "You all had parents until you were teenagers! You all get to remember Mom and Dad. And you remember little family stories. And you have gifts to look at and remember Mom's lectures."

Julia and Charlie looked totally confused.

"Well, it's not fair!" I said. "I don't have parents! So I don't have any family memories, and I don't know anything about my relatives, and now I don't even have a big twelfth-birthday present like everyone else."

I choked down a sob.

"Cla-dee?" Owen asked. He sounded scared—he's not used to me yelling.

"And what about Owen?" I exploded. "He has even less than I do. He doesn't even have a baby book! And none of you cares!"

I snatched up Owen's album and my social studies notes and ran upstairs.

"Claudia!" Charlie called after me. I heard Owen start to cry.

I slammed my bedroom door behind me and burst into tears.

chapter ten

"Thanks a lot," I called to the city bus driver. I climbed off the bus right in front of the mall.

I wasn't supposed to meet Jody for another hour. But I couldn't stand sitting around in the house—not when I was so upset. How could Julia and Charlie act like this twelfth-birthday thing was no big deal?

I could just picture Mom handing me some important family gift—something beautiful and special—anything. And I could practically hear her voice, telling me how important it was, how I should take care of it. It just wasn't fair!

Inside the mall, the stores were just opening up. Since I had time to kill before Jody got there, I went into

Lamm's Department Store first. It was the first time I'd been there since Jody took the earrings for me.

I kept my eyes down while I scooted past the jewelry counter.

There were some new bookbags in the back that looked pretty nice. Other than that, though, Lamm's was boring.

I bought some pistachio nuts at the health food store and wandered toward Mason's. It was almost ten-thirty. I finished my pistachios, chucked the bag in the trash, and went into Mason's.

First I spent a few minutes in lingerie, checking out the bras and stuff. I like to do this when no one else is looking—I'm a little self-conscious about my size. I mean, I don't even really *have* a size yet.

Next I hit the juniors department. I started with a section called Young Casuals and looked at denim overalls. Next I moved on to striped T-shirts. Nothing looked interesting. I wasn't really in the mood to shop. I just kept thinking about how I never got a special twelfth birthday present.

A salesperson moved past.

"Excuse me? Do you know what time it is?" I asked.

She checked her watch. "Ten fifty-five."

Time to go. I didn't want to be late to meet Jody—not that she would care. I just have a thing about being on time.

I squeezed past a rack of bathing suits and took a shortcut through jackets. Then suddenly I stopped.

On the rack in front of me was the coolest jacket I'd ever seen in my life. I pulled it off the rack and held it up. It was denim, with daisies embroidered on the collar and sleeves.

I couldn't believe what an amazing jacket I'd found. It was totally perfect.

I took it off the hanger and put it on.

It fit perfectly—even the sleeves fit! Sleeves are usually too long on me.

I walked over to the mirror and checked myself out. It looked great!

This jacket is too cool, I thought. I have to buy it.

I held up my arm and checked out the price tag swinging from the cuff.

Ninety-five dollars.

Whoa! No way! I could never afford that!

I was totally bummed. How many times did I find something I really, really loved? Hardly ever.

I took the jacket off and started to put it back.

But I really want it! I thought. It's totally perfect.

I glanced around. Nobody was nearby. No salespeople. No customers. No security guards.

Jody would just take the jacket, I thought. Kelly would just take it.

I remembered yesterday, how easy it was to take the lip gloss.

No way, I thought. I can't shoplift. I hung up the jacket and started to walk away. But that jacket was so cool. It looked so good on me.

Maybe I'll try it on again, I thought. I edged back over to the rack. I'll just put it on and look at it some more.

Could I get Charlie to give me money for this jacket? I wondered. No—he already told Bailey money was tight this month.

It's not fair, I thought. I deserve something special— just like Charlie, Bailey, and Julia.

I stared into the mirror. I really want this jacket, I thought. I don't have anything else. Why shouldn't I just take this jacket?

I glanced at my watch. I was late to meet Jody!

Jody would take the jacket if she wanted it. She would just tie the jacket around her waist so the tags didn't show.

No salespeople were around. The store was totally quiet.

I quickly took off the jacket and tied it around my waist.

Did anyone see me?

I waited a few seconds. All I could hear was the pounding of my heart.

No one came after me.

I casually walked out of the juniors department and started for the shoe department on the second floor.

Jody was right all along, I thought. This is really easy. Nobody even noticed me!

Smiling, I climbed onto the escalator and hurried to meet Jody.

chapter eleven

I saw Jody before she saw me. She was standing in front of the shoe department, pacing back and forth.

I snuck up behind her. "Boo!"

Jody jumped and turned around. "So where were you?"

I was so excited about my new jacket that I was about to burst. "Sorry. I had to, um, *pick something up.*" I motioned to the jacket tied around my waist.

Jody's eyes grew big. "No!"

She was impressed. I could tell.

"Yes," I said. "Five-finger discount. No one noticed me."

"Why should they?" Jody said. "You have such a sweet, innocent face. Nobody would ever suspect you."

"It was so easy, Jody," I went on. "I couldn't believe it. I just, you know, tied it around my waist and walked away!"

Jody kept staring at me with this big grin on her face. "I can't believe you, Fiddle Girl. This is really cool."

She sounded surprised. So I decided to act casual about it. I would show Jody that it was no big thing. She could come to the mall and have fun with me, just like she did with Kelly.

"Wait a minute," I said. "Where's Kelly?"

Jody shrugged. "I don't know. I called her this morning, but she never called back."

"Oh." I glanced around the shoe department. "Did you find any boots you like?"

"Nah. This place stinks. I want to go to the Sports Attic. Kelly told me they have cool hiking boots there."

"Let's go," I said.

We headed down the escalator to the first floor of Mason's. I couldn't stop smiling. I was so happy with my new jacket.

Jody glanced sideways at me. "We should make a stop before we go out into the mall."

"Why?"

Jody turned into the ladies' room. "To get rid of those tags on your jacket," she whispered.

I gasped. "You're right. I never thought about that."

Jody laughed. "Well, think about it. Sometimes they

put magnetized tags on things. It sets off the alarm when you try to leave."

"So what do you do then?"

"You don't take it," she answered. "The cashiers have special tools to get those tags off. You can't take them off yourself."

"Wow," I said. "I almost walked right out of the store with this! I could have gotten caught!"

"Relax, Claud," Jody said. "They usually only put the tags on expensive stuff."

There was no one in the bathroom. I took off the jacket, and Jody checked it over.

"Only paper tags," she announced. She used her teeth to cut the string, then threw the tags into the toilet.

I flushed them down.

"Now the jacket's yours," Jody told me.

"I forgot how huge this place is," I said when we reached the Sports Attic.

"And how popular," Jody added.

I looked around. She was right—the place was packed. Suddenly I noticed a sign at the back of the store—a sign for Emmitt Smith special edition footballs.

The football Bailey wanted.

He *really* wants one, I thought. I untied the new jacket from around my waist and slipped it on.

It was so easy to take the jacket, I thought. Maybe I should just take a football for Bailey.

I grabbed Jody's arm. "I need to pick something up here," I told her.

She stared at me in surprise. "You want to take something else?"

I nodded. "A football."

"A *football?*" Jody's eyebrows shot up. "What for?"

"For Bailey. He really wants this special football to impress his friends at college. He'll be so happy if I get it for him."

"Oh. Okay," Jody said slowly. "But I think a football will be a little tricky to lift, Claud."

"No way," I said. "I can do it. No problem."

Jody shook her head. "Okay—you're the expert," she teased me.

"Will you help?" I asked.

"Sure."

I led her to the Emmitt Smiths. They were right beside the in-line skates department. The footballs had their own special display and a sign saying "NEW!"

Jody glanced at the price tag. "Whoa! A hundred dollars. These are way expensive, Claud," she whispered. "No wonder Bailey couldn't afford one."

"That's what makes it a good present," I whispered back.

Jody looked a little nervous. "I've never taken anything that expensive," she admitted. "Even Kelly doesn't take things like this."

I smiled. Now Jody could tell Kelly stories about *me*. But still, I began to feel a little bit nervous. If Jody couldn't do this, how could I?

"Is the coast clear?" Jody asked.

No one seemed to be working in the football section, but there was a guy stationed by the Rollerblades. "Not exactly," I told her. I jerked my head in his direction.

"Mmmm," Jody said.

I glanced around. Jody was right—this wouldn't be easy. I would have to take the football without anyone seeing me. No problem. But then I would have to walk through the entire store with a huge football under my jacket.

"We need a plan," Jody said. "Got any ideas?"

I shook my head.

Jody gestured toward the salesman near the Roller-blades. "He's the biggest problem."

"Besides the fact that a football is kind of hard not to notice," I joked.

Jody laughed. "I could distract the salesman," she offered. "Then you wrap the football inside your jacket and leave."

"Okay," I said. "Let's go."

"I can't believe we're doing this," Jody said. But she was smiling as she made her way over to the salesman.

"Excuse me," she called. "Can you help me?"

He smiled. "Sure."

Jody led him over to the far side of the Rollerblade display. "Could you tell me what other colors these come in?"

"Uh, only the colors you see here."

"O-kay," Jody said. "I guess I can live with purple and orange together. So . . . do these come with any kind of guarantee? You know, in case you crash and wreck them?"

I turned back to the footballs. Slowly I took off the jacket and put it over my arm.

"Has anyone ever had a wheel fall off?" I heard Jody ask.

I moved in front of the footballs and reached out.

"Honey, have you seen these new Emmitt Smiths?"

Yikes! I jumped back just as a middle-aged couple came up next to me.

What was I supposed to do now? I couldn't take the football with these people standing here! Jody would have to keep the sales guy talking until they left.

I glanced over at Jody. She shot me an I-can't-do-this-much-longer look. I gestured toward the couple, and she rolled her eyes.

"So . . . which of these cause the fewest blisters?" she asked. "Let's start at the very top of the shelf."

I tried to keep from laughing. Jody could keep that

guy talking all day if she wanted to. I picked up a blue football helmet and pretended to examine it while I waited for the couple to leave.

They just stood there, talking about whether the football was too expensive to buy for their son.

Come *on,* I thought. Just leave!

"But what if I wear them *without* socks?" I heard Jody ask.

I glanced back at the couple. Finally! They were moving toward the helmets. Casually I switched places with them.

They turned their backs to me while they studied a helmet. No one else was watching.

I put my hand on one of the footballs.

"Let's get the salesman over here," the man said.

Oh, no! I snatched my hand away. Not the salesman! How could I ever take the football with *him* in this section?

Why don't those people just get out of here?

"Excuse me," the man called over to Jody's salesman. "Are you busy?"

Jody jumped in front of him. She pointed at the Rollerblades. "I'd like to try this one, this one, this one, and this one in size five, please," she announced. "And I want all of them in black *and* in purple."

The salesman sighed. "I'll be with you in a minute," he called to the man near me.

I stared at the couple. Please just leave, I thought. Please!

The woman seemed frustrated. "Maybe we should come back when the store isn't as crowded," she said.

"Good idea," her husband answered. They turned and walked away.

Yes! Jody did it! She actually drove them away.

"Psst!" I looked at Jody. She jumped up and down, pointing at the footballs. The salesman wasn't back yet. We were all alone.

Quickly I grabbed a football off the shelf. I eased my jacket over it.

Jody collapsed onto the bench in the skate department.

Hunching my body over my jacket, I tiptoed down the football aisle. So far, so good. The football felt huge, though. Much bigger than I'd expected. How was I ever going to make it out of the store?

The football slipped down. I could feel it sinking. It was about to drop on the floor.

I quickly bent over to keep the football from falling. But how could I pick it back up without anyone noticing?

I was practically bent over double. And then I saw them—a pair of feet standing right in front of me.

A salesman! Where did he come from? Had he seen me take the football? My heart started to pound.

"Miss, are you okay?" he asked. He held two big Rollerblade boxes.

I hunched even tighter so he wouldn't notice the football. Oh, no! Now what?

"Uh . . . just bad cramps," I mumbled.

"Watch out!" someone yelled. The salesman spun around just as Jody came barreling around the corner on Rollerblades. She grabbed on to a shelf to steady herself. "Help! How do you stop on these things?" she screamed.

The guy dropped his boxes and ran over to catch her.

I couldn't believe it. Jody had saved me again! I turned and rushed out of the football section. I didn't stop walking until I made it through the front door and into the mall.

I went right into the ladies' room near the food court.

Jody caught up with me a few minutes later. I was still hunched over, trying to calm myself down.

"I don't believe you," she said.

"I don't believe *you*," I answered. "That poor guy must have thought you were crazy."

We looked at each other and burst out laughing.

"What else could I do?" Jody asked. "I had to get him away from you, right?" She pointed to my stomach. "You look like you have a stomachache."

"I do," I said. "I'm about to have a football."

Jody laughed again. "Claudia—I can't believe you really did it!"

"Thank you, thank you," I said. I pulled the football out from under my jacket. "But what am I supposed to do with it now?"

Jody was already rummaging through the trash. She pulled out an old shopping bag. "Here! Stuff it in."

The football fit perfectly.

I put my new jacket back on. This was turning out to be the best trip to the mall ever. I had a cool new jacket, *and* I had a great present for Bailey.

"Now what?" Jody asked.

"Home," I said. "I can't wait to give Bailey his present."

chapter twelve

"Hi, Claud," Bailey said. "What's up?"

He stood in the basement, folding laundry.

"I'm so happy you're here," I said. I held the football hidden behind my back.

Bailey looked confused. "Why?"

I bounced up and down in excitement. "Close your eyes and put out your hands," I answered.

"What for?"

"Because . . . because . . ." I tried not to giggle. "Just do it, okay?"

"Okay," Bailey said. He closed his eyes and stuck out his hands. I put the football on them. "For you."

Bailey opened his eyes and gave a little gasp. "An

Emmitt Smith? I-I don't get it. Where did you get this? What is it for?"

"It's for you!" I said. "A little present from me."

"A *little* present? Claudia—are you sure? This is . . ." He turned the football over in his hands. "This is more than a little present, Claudia. Where did you get the money for this?"

Oops. I didn't think he would ask *that*. An uneasy feeling began to grow in my stomach. I hadn't even thought about what Bailey would say when I gave him the football.

"I, um, saved up," I told him. "I've been saving my allowance for months. I wasn't sure how I wanted to spend it, but when I saw the footballs at the mall . . ."

Bailey shook his head. "Are you sure you want me to have it?"

"Yes," I said. "I wanted to do something special for you. I know how much you wanted it."

Bailey put the football on top of the dryer. Then he reached over to give me a huge hug. "Claudia, I can't believe you would do something this wonderful!"

I was feeling worse and worse. "It's no big deal."

"Yes, it is. It's a big deal that you would spend your own money on something for me." He shook his head. "It really means a lot to me, Claud."

I let Bailey hug me. I was happy he liked the football so much. But suddenly I felt terrible. I mean, Bailey assumed that I *bought* the football. He thought it was really special because I *bought* it.

Only I didn't buy it.

It's still a present, I told myself. I still got it especially for Bailey—even if I didn't actually spend money on it.

Besides, it's not like the football was *easy* to get.

It was really hard to get.

That doesn't matter, I thought as I climbed the stairs to the kitchen. I can't believe I gave him a stolen football. It was so exciting to shoplift that I didn't even think about what Bailey would say.

I went up to my room and hid my new jacket in the back of my closet. Then I lay on the bed. A picture of Mom and Dad was propped on the night table.

I studied it for a minute. And then I realized something really important. I was jealous of my brothers and sister because they had special gifts from Mom and Dad, and I didn't.

But a cool jacket didn't help one bit.

I missed Mom and Dad so much. And not all the shoplifting in the world would make that sadness go away.

chapter thirteen

"Claudia! Phone!"

Bailey's voice woke me up on Sunday morning.

"Claud? It's Jody!"

I climbed out of bed and stumbled down the stairs. Bailey met me at the bottom, holding out the cordless phone.

"Crashed on the couch again, huh?" I asked him.

"Mmmph," he mumbled. I don't think he was really awake yet. I took the phone into the kitchen.

"Hello?"

"Want to go to the mall again?" Jody asked. "Mom has to go out in about ten minutes so she said she'd drop us off."

"Well—"

"The only thing is, we have to take the bus home," Jody interrupted.

The thought of taking the bus didn't thrill me. But spending more time with Jody did.

"Is Kelly coming?" I asked.

"No," Jody said. "I haven't talked to her in two days."

Charlie came into the kitchen carrying Owen in one arm and a shopping bag in the other. "Can I go to the mall with Jody?" I asked.

Charlie unloaded Owen and the shopping bag onto the floor. "Again? Weren't you just there yesterday?"

"Yeah," I said. "So?"

Charlie shrugged. "How long will you be gone?"

"I don't know. Maybe an hour or two? Please? There's nothing to do here."

Charlie laughed. "That's easy for you to say." He reached down and took a bottle of aspirin away from Owen, who had discovered it in the shopping bag.

"Please?" I said again.

"Okay," he answered. "But don't be long. I don't want you to turn into a mall rat, Claudia."

"Yeah, right," I said, laughing. "I can come," I told Jody.

"I heard," Jody answered. "Wait for me outside. Mom and I will be by in about fifteen minutes."

* * *

Mrs. Lynch was right on time. I don't see Jody's mother much. I guess that's because she's always working. Jody complains a lot about having to hang out by herself at home. I don't know what her problem is—I'd *love* to have peace and quiet at home!

Mrs. Lynch looks a lot like Jody—only with blond hair instead of red. Jody said her mom used to be a ballet dancer when she was young.

She pulled up to the curb. "Hi, Claudia. Hop in."

"Thanks," I said, sliding into the backseat.

Mrs. Lynch took off. "So . . . two trips to the mall in one weekend," she said.

"Yeah, I know," I answered. "My brother is worried we're turning into mall rats."

Mrs. Lynch laughed.

"Mom," Jody said. "Can me and Claud have lunch at the mall?"

"Sorry, Jody. Can't," I said. "I have to get home and finish my social studies project."

"You can't, either," Mrs. Lynch told Jody. "You're spending the afternoon at Grandma Betty and Pop Bill's house."

"Oh, gross," Jody groaned. "They're so boring. All they ever want to do is watch old movies. Yuck."

"Maybe they can help you with your family history project," I suggested.

Bad move. Jody looked at me as if I were crazy. "Are

you kidding? If I asked them a question about our family history, they'd never shut up."

"Duh, Jody—that's the whole point. How else will you ever learn about your relatives?"

Jody shrugged.

"You're lucky," I told her. "At least you have grand-parents to ask."

"Yeah, but who cares?" Jody said. "I don't need to know all those boring stories."

Mrs. Lynch pulled up in front of the mall. We climbed out of the car. "When will you be home?" Mrs. Lynch called through the window.

"How should I know?" Jody answered. She's always rude to her mother. I think she does it to get attention. At least, that's what Julia would say.

"Noon," her mother answered. "Any later and you're in big trouble, okay?"

"Yeah, yeah," Jody said, walking off.

"Bye, Mrs. Lynch. Thanks!" I called. I ran to catch up with Jody.

She was holding open the mall door for me. "Wow," I said. "Do you always talk to your mom like that?"

Jody shrugged. "She's always on my case."

"Yeah, but . . . she's your mom."

"Let's go to Mason's," Jody said, changing the sub-ject. "We'll check out the designer department. Every-thing is really expensive, but it's fun to look anyway."

"Sounds good to me."

We checked out the leather jackets first. But they all had wire cables attached to them so you couldn't even try them on.

Next we looked at fancy dresses. Stuff you would wear to a formal dance or something. Jody pulled a strapless black dress off the rack. "You should get this for your next recital, Claud," she joked.

Whenever I perform with my violin, I always have to look really nice.

"I wish!" I laughed. "It would probably slide right off me."

Jody moved over to the next aisle. "These are nice." She flipped through a rack of cute summer dresses.

I followed her and started flipping through them.

"This one's your size," Jody observed. "You should take it."

It was a pretty orange slip dress. Not really my favorite color, but very short and cute. It didn't look little girl-y, either, like a lot of my other clothes.

Jody went over to another rack nearby and started working her way through.

The orange dress *was* nice—nice enough, anyway. I kind of liked it. And nobody was around.

I had a lot of fun yesterday. I hated to admit it—but shoplifting had been kind of exciting.

I glanced down at the dress.

It was really thin and light. No one would even notice if I stuffed it under my sweater.

But shoplifting didn't really make me feel better, I thought. Not once I got home, anyway.

The dress felt silky in my hand.

I guess I might feel a *little* bit happier if I had this dress, I thought.

It slid right off the hanger. And under my sweater. It only took a second. Easy.

Casually I walked over to Jody. "Let's go," I whispered.

She shot me a curious look. "Why?"

"I have something new to show you," I whispered.

"You took something?" she whispered back. "I can't believe you!"

She followed me to the front door. I could hardly wait to get out into the mall so I could show Jody the dress.

"Excuse me, miss," a stern voice commanded. "Please stop right there."

chapter fourteen

Stay where you are," the security guard said.

I froze. My heart slammed against my rib cage. Oh, no, I thought. This can't be happening.

Oh, no, oh, no, oh, no!

What were they going to do to me?

I slowly turned around.

On the other side of the rack, the security guard stood in front of a girl about my age. "Let me see what you have there," he demanded.

My knees felt weak. It wasn't me! He didn't catch me! I felt so relieved, I could hardly breathe. I just stood there, staring at the guard.

"Claudia," Jody whispered. "Move!"

I couldn't move. I was still too scared. That was so close! So awful!

Jody grabbed my sleeve and pulled me over behind a huge rack of backpacks. We watched the guard from there.

"Come on," he said. "What's under your coat?"

"Nothing," the girl squeaked. She turned toward us, trying to move away from the guard.

"No way!" Jody whispered in horror. "It's Shannon Wilson!"

I gasped. Shannon from school.

"Let's see it," the guard ordered.

Shannon looked totally terrified—as if she was about to burst into tears. Slowly she pulled a sweater out from underneath her jacket.

The store manager appeared beside the guard. "You'll have to come with us, please," the manager said.

Shannon panicked. "Wait!" she cried. "Where are we going?"

"To call the police," the manager told her.

Now Shannon *did* start crying. "But . . . how about if I just put the sweater back?" she begged.

The guard and the manager both shook their heads. "Sorry," the guard said, taking her elbow. "You have to come with us, miss."

She pulled back. "I can't! I can't go with you. My

parents will kill me. Can't I just put the sweater back? Please?"

The manager shook her head. "Store policy."

"No!" Shannon shrieked. "No! Please! I promise I won't do it ever again."

The guard took her firmly by the elbow and steered her toward the manager's office. Shannon sobbed all the way there.

I couldn't stop shaking. I stared down at the dress I'd just lifted. Was I crazy? That could have been *me!*

What if I'd gotten caught? What would my family think? And the whole school would know. How would I ever face my teachers? My friends?

I was a thief!

No wonder shoplifting didn't make me feel any better, I thought. Because I'm a thief!

I slid the dress out from under my sweater and let it drop to the floor.

Jody watched me, her eyes wide. "Let's go!" she whispered.

We ducked down and got out of there.

Once we were back out in the mall, we finally spoke. "Bad news in there," Jody said.

"Yeah," I answered. "Poor Shannon." I could still picture the tears running down her cheeks. "What do you think's going to happen to her?"

Jody shrugged. "I don't want to think about it."

"Me, neither," I said.

But I couldn't help it. It was all I could think about. People *do* get caught. *I* could have gotten caught! I was in the same store, doing the same thing.

In school Shannon had said you didn't get in trouble if the store caught you. She said they just made you put back whatever you took.

But that wasn't true. They called the *police!*

I would never shoplift again. Never.

I turned to Jody.

"Where to now?" she asked.

"I want to go home," I answered.

chapter fifteen

Owen's first video . . ." I chewed on the end of my pen while I tried to remember.

But it was useless. I pushed the baby book to the side of my bed and rolled over onto my back. "Owen's first visit to Claudia in jail," I whispered. "That's more like it."

I stared at my bedroom ceiling. I was supposed to be working on my social studies project before dinner. But I couldn't stop feeling guilty.

I sat up and stared at Owen's baby book. I can't believe it, I thought. I'm a criminal.

How could I have just gone around *stealing* things? How would I feel if Charlie had to come pick me up at the police station? How could Owen ever look up to me again if he knew I was a thief?

Even worse, what would Social Services say if the police called them? They would think I was a juvenile delinquent. They would take me away from Charlie and send me to some horrible foster home.

They could even send Owen away.

How could I have done this? It's so important that we do everything right. I mean, we don't have parents watching out for us. And the social workers would blame *Charlie* if I got caught stealing things.

Why didn't I think of that? Wasn't that more important than having a really cool jacket?

And the worst part was, it *wasn't* Charlie's fault I was stealing things. It was *my* fault.

I did it because I felt sorry for myself. And because I was afraid I would lose my best friend.

"And because I'm an idiot," I whispered. Stealing was selfish, and wrong, and just . . . dumb. All the things Mom and Dad always told me.

I wanted to fix what I'd done. Make everything the way it was before. But what could I do about it now?

Should I confess to Charlie? What would he say? What *could* he say?

How could I ever have done this to my family?

And how was I ever going to fix it?

I rolled off the bed and picked up Owen's book. It was due tomorrow. I absolutely had to finish it tonight.

I headed down to the kitchen with the book tucked under my arm. I only had a few more things to fill in. I plunked myself down at the table and tried to concentrate on Owen's memories.

Slowly I leafed through the book. Even without anyone's help, it looked great. Owen would be proud of it. So would Mom and Dad.

I started filling in the last few pages: "My favorite things to do."

Hmmm. What about watching cartoons on TV? I put it down. *Singing songs,* I added. *Especially songs about dogs.*

I went on to the next page: "My Second Birthday." I had found one of the party invitations in Owen's room. It had a big green lizard on the front, and when you opened it up it said, "Owen is two. Come celebrate!"

He had a great party. Julia and I thought up all these games like pin the tail on the lizard and jungle treasure hunt. We had a blast. Even if Owen did like the wrapping paper better than the presents.

I pasted the invitation into his book and filled in as many details as I could remember. The guests, the presents, the party favors.

I flipped to the next page—"My Third Birthday." But that wasn't for a while yet.

"I'm finished!" I said aloud. I already felt a lot better than I had when I got home from the mall. I really did it! Owen had a book now, just like the rest of us.

Julia wandered into the kitchen. Owen trailed behind her. He had on his choo-choo train pajamas.

"More juice?" he asked.

"What kind do you want?" Julia answered. "Apple or cherry?"

Owen stopped for a minute and thought. He looked adorable. His hair was all messed up from sleeping on it funny. "Both."

Julia laughed. "You have to pick *one,* Owen. Apple or cherry?"

"Cherry," he said. Then he noticed me. "Cla-dee!" he yelled.

"Hi, O-ee," I said.

He padded over to the table. I hoisted him up onto my lap. "I made a book about you. Do you want to see it?"

Owen nodded.

Julia brought Owen his juice. "Oh, wow. You filled in Owen's baby book?"

"Yep," I said proudly. "Look."

We started at the beginning. "Here's you right after you were born," I told Owen.

Owen burst out laughing.

"Oh! Let me see," Julia said. She stared at the picture.

"Look, O. Here's Mommy and Daddy. . . . Isn't Mommy pretty?" Her voice got a little sad.

"And look at all the cards people sent you," I said, quickly flipping the page. "See all the cards? You must have been very popular!"

Owen clapped his hands together. "What that?"

"It's called a family tree," I explained. "It shows who your parents and grandparents and great-grandparents are."

Julia pointed to Alonzo Phelps, our great-grandfather. "This guy was a traveling piano salesman."

"He was?" I asked. "I never knew that!"

Julia nodded. "Mom told me about Grandpa Lon. He rode up and down the Mississippi on a paddlewheel boat." Julia studied the family tree. "And his wife, Elizabeth Phelps, was a concert pianist. Did you know that?"

"No!"

Julia laughed. "Where do you think you get your musical talent?"

"From Mom?"

"Right. And where did she get it?"

"From her grandmother Elizabeth. Wow."

Julia looked at me for a moment. "You really care about this stuff, don't you?" she asked. "Stories about our relatives, I mean."

I nodded. "I don't even remember much about Mom

114

and Dad," I explained. "And I don't know *anything* about our other relatives. Sometimes I just feel like I don't even have a family."

Julia frowned. "Well, you do," she said. "And now that I know how important it is, I'll tell you everything I know about our relatives. Everything Mom and Dad ever told me."

I smiled at her. "Thanks, Jules."

"Turn the page!" Owen demanded.

"Sorry." We went on to Owen's "Memorable Firsts."

"What this?" he asked.

"It tells when you first crawled. When you first walked. Your first words . . ."

Owen giggled.

"I remember when you took your first steps, O," Julia said. "You were standing right here in the kitchen."

"I didn't know that," I complained.

"You were at Jeff's house," Julia told me. "Don't you remember how mad you were that you missed it?"

I nodded. "Sort of."

Julia hugged Owen. "You took two steps and fell back on your bottom," she told him. "Boom!"

Owen thought that was hilarious.

Bailey and Charlie appeared in the doorway.

"What's so funny?" Charlie asked.

"Claudia finished Owen's baby book," Julia said. "Come see. It's really terrific!"

Everyone crowded around the table. I flipped back to page one and started over again.

"Cool family tree," Charlie said. He pointed to the great-grandfather named Benjamin Salinger. "He started the first Salinger's."

"He did?"

"It was a hot-dog stand on the corner of Market and Fifth. Best hot dogs in San Francisco."

"I know which guy you mean," Bailey interrupted. "There's an old photo of him hanging in the restaurant."

"The guy with the hot-dog truck!" I said. It was a small framed photo of a guy with a hat and a handlebar mustache. "I never knew he was anyone *important*."

"I have his gold money clip," Bailey said.

"I know. You got it for your big twelfth-birthday present," I answered.

I saw Charlie and Julia glance at each other. I felt embarrassed. They probably thought I would get upset and storm off again.

"Um, Claud," Charlie said. "Speaking of twelfth birthday presents . . ."

"We thought you should have one," Julia finished for him. "We felt really lousy about what happened yesterday. I mean, we never even thought about it."

"Mom and Dad would have remembered to give you something," Charlie put in. "But without them here, none of us realized how important it is to tell you about the family history."

"It is important, though," Bailey said. "Because someday we'll have to tell Owen about these weird people on his family tree. We all have to remember."

Julia opened a cabinet near the pantry and pulled out a long skinny box. It was covered in black velvet.

She handed it to me. "Charlie and I went down to the bank and took out the safe-deposit box," she told me. "The rest of us all got something from Mom's or Dad's relatives. But we thought you should have something of Mom's."

I opened the velvet box and peered inside. Pearls. A long string of beautiful pearls. My eyes filled with tears. "Mom is wearing these in the picture I have of her," I whispered. "The concert picture I keep in my violin case."

Charlie put his arm around my shoulders. "I know we can't take their place, Claud," he said. "But at least we can give you a special twelfth-birthday present like they would have. I hope you like it."

"Even if it is almost a year late," Bailey added.

I laughed. "Thanks, you guys. I'll wear these to all my violin recitals from now on."

"Book!" Owen yelled.

"Oops! Sorry, O," I said. We continued through the book.

"This is really great, Claudia," Charlie told me. "How did you ever figure all this out?"

"Well—"

"Wait a second," Charlie cut in. "I take that back. First word . . . *Claudia?*"

"That wasn't Owen's first word!" Bailey said. "It was *og,* for *dog.*"

I smiled. "Prove it."

"First tooth, one month?" Julia said. "Try *six* months, Claud."

"Owen was an advanced baby," I told her.

Charlie laughed. He flipped through the rest of the book. "Good job, Claud," he said. "I am very impressed."

"Me, too," Bailey said.

"So," I said. "I did this for my social studies project. But Owen's baby book goes until he gets to first grade— and I think we should keep his book up-to-date until it's finished. Don't you?"

"Absolutely," Charlie said.

"No question," Bailey added.

Julia nodded. "I think," she said slowly, "I owe you an apology, Claud. Mom and Dad would have liked this book. Now that they're gone, it's up to us to keep our family history going."

"Thanks," I said.

Julia bent down to tickle Owen's tummy. "Isn't that right, O?"

He squealed.

"Hey! I have the best idea," Julia cried. "Stay there, guys. Don't anyone move."

She disappeared upstairs.

Two seconds later she was back, carrying her camera. "Let's start updating family memories right now. Owen: two and a half, with his family."

She started pulling out chairs from the kitchen table. "Charlie, you sit here with Owen on your lap. Bailey, next to Charlie."

Julia arranged us and rearranged us until we looked just right. Then she set the automatic timer and ran to take her place in the picture.

"Say 'family,'" she called out.

"Family!" we all yelled.

I clutched my new pearls and smiled. I felt better now that I had a twelfth-birthday present. And some more family memories. And a great sister and great brothers.

But something was still wrong.

I was a thief. And I had to fix that.

What was I going to do about the stuff I stole?

chapter sixteen

After dinner that night I wandered down to the basement to think. Bailey's new Emmitt Smith football was still sitting on the dryer. I stared at it for a long time. Bailey had been so excited when I gave it to him. He wanted that football so much, and I wanted to be the one to make him happy.

Upstairs, I heard my brothers and sister get up from the table. I heard Bailey tell everyone good night as he left for his apartment.

"Bye, Claud!" he yelled. Then I heard Julia say, "Time for bed, O."

I climbed back upstairs and went straight to my room. I opened the closet door and pulled out my new denim jacket.

Carefully I laid it out on my bed. Taking the jacket had been so *thrilling*. And I loved the jacket. But it wasn't mine. It didn't belong to me. I hadn't paid for it.

And my family would be so disappointed if they ever found out that I had stolen it.

Right then I knew what I had to do to make things okay again: I had to return the jacket.

And the music note earrings and necklace Jody gave me.

I grabbed a sheet of notebook paper from my desk and wrote: "Dear Mason's Department Store: I took this jacket without paying for it. Sorry. A Customer." Then I put the note into a shopping bag along with the jacket.

Right away I felt better. I was doing the right thing.

I wrote another note to Lamm's—even though *Jody* had taken the music note jewelry. I knew she would never take something back to the store, so I would do it for her.

But there was still something else—Bailey's football. What could I do about that? It meant so much to him. Wasn't there any way he could keep it?

Maybe I could pay for it—just like I told him I did. I dumped my piggy bank out on the bed and counted up all the money. Grand total: $23.16.

Great. That was nowhere near a hundred dollars! I slumped down on my bed. What should I do?

I had to return the football. But if I did, I would have to tell Bailey why I took his present back. And that was going to be hard. *Really* hard. Until now, I was just disappointed with myself. But if I told Bailey what I did . . .

I would disappoint him, too.

Plus, he might tell Charlie and Julia that I stole it! I didn't want anyone in my family to know that.

I have no choice, I thought. I have to take it back. I'll just have to make Bailey understand. I'll make him promise not to tell anyone else.

I tiptoed out of my room. The house was quiet. Owen was already in bed for the night. Downstairs, Julia and Charlie were watching TV.

They didn't notice me as I crept down to the basement. Bailey's football still sat on the dryer. I tucked it under my arm and carried it back to my room.

I sat down on the bed and took out a third sheet of paper. "Dear Sports Attic: I took this and it didn't belong to me. Sorry. A Customer."

When I was finished, I added the football to the shopping bag. Then I crawled under my covers, closed my eyes, and went to sleep.

Tomorrow I would fix everything.

* * *

The next day after school I went straight to the mall.

First I went to Lamm's. I just sort of dropped the music note jewelry onto a counter while no one was looking.

Next, I took my shopping bag with the note and jacket inside and left them right inside the front door of Mason's. I made sure none of the security guards was around to see me. Then I walked away really fast.

Already, I felt better.

I headed for the Sports Attic next. When I got to the entrance, I tucked the football by the side of the front door. I hoped a guard would find it right away. I didn't want anyone else to take it.

Then I practically ran outside. I got on the bus and headed for home.

There—I did it!

Now I just had to tell Bailey. He would understand. Wouldn't he?

"You did what?" Bailey shouted.

I stared down at my sneakers. "I sort of . . . took the football without paying for it first."

I peeked up at Bailey. He sat on the living room couch with his mouth hanging open. He didn't say a word.

Neither did I.

"You mean you stole it?" he exploded suddenly. "Claudia, you *stole* the football for me?"

I felt tears rush to my eyes. Bailey had never yelled at me like that before. "Well, yes. But then I decided that wasn't a good idea, so I returned it to the store."

I don't think he even heard me. "Why would you steal something, Claudia?" he screamed. "Why would you even *think* of stealing something?"

"I didn't really think I was *stealing*," I tried to explain. I knew it sounded lame. "I mean, it was shoplifting. Everybody does it."

Bailey shook his head. "That is the stupidest, most immature thing I have ever heard!" he shouted. "I am really disappointed in you, Claudia."

Now I was getting mad. Bailey wasn't even paying attention to me! He was just yelling and waving his arms around.

"Hey, I returned it, okay?" I said loudly. "How about some credit here for doing the right thing?"

"What would have happened if you got caught?" he demanded. "Did you even think about that? Or were you just thinking about yourself?"

"No! I was thinking about *you!*" I yelled. "I got it for *you!*"

Bailey rolled his eyes. "Oh, come on, Claudia. I'm not stupid. If you took that football, I know you took things for yourself, too."

I gasped. Why was he talking to me this way? Didn't he realize I was *apologizing?*

124

"I'm not a little kid, you know!" I cried. "I already figured this whole thing out. It's taken care of, okay?"

Bailey stood up and started pacing. "Why would you even think I'd *want* something you stole?"

"What is your problem, Bailey?" I shouted. "I already told you, I took it back!"

"Claudia!" Julia yelled. "Phone! It's Jody."

I glared at Bailey. Then I stomped upstairs.

Bailey followed me. "Claudia! What are you doing? What do you think you're doing?"

"Hello?" I said into the hall phone.

"What's going on over there?" Jody asked.

Bailey was standing practically on top of me. I pushed him away. "Nothing."

"Do you want to go to the mall again today?" Jody asked. "I'm totally bored."

I looked straight at Bailey. "Sure, Jody," I said loudly. "I'd love to go to the mall."

Bailey's face turned red. I've never seen him look so angry.

"I'll meet you in front of Mason's in half an hour," I told Jody. I slammed the phone down.

"Are you crazy?" Bailey shouted. "What do you think you're doing?"

"Minding my own business," I snapped. "You should try it."

I stomped into my room and slammed the door.

"This *is* my business!" he yelled. I could hear him stomp back downstairs. The front door banged shut.

I opened my door and grabbed my backpack. I didn't need some stupid brother to tell me how to live my life.

I would be much happier hanging out with my best friend.

chapter seventeen

Jody was waiting for me in front of Mason's. "What's wrong?" she asked. "You look mad."

"I don't want to talk about it," I muttered. I don't get mad that easily, but I was mad now. I couldn't believe Bailey! He thought I was still a thief even after I took back all the stolen stuff!

If he thinks I'm a thief, I told myself, maybe I should just *be* a thief!

"Where's Kelly?" I asked Jody.

"Haven't I told you?" Jody said. "She and Wiley made up. They're back together."

"You're kidding!" I thought about that for a second. If Wiley and Kelly were back together, that meant Kelly wouldn't be hanging around anymore.

Things between Jody and me could go back to normal. It was the first good news I'd had all day. "I guess we won't be seeing much of her anymore, huh?"

"You got that right," Jody said. "She's history now. It's too bad—Kelly's a lot of fun."

I wasn't so sure about that, but I didn't say anything to Jody. "So . . . where should we go?"

"I still want to find some boots," Jody said. "Who else do you think sells cool boots?"

I thought for a minute. "I know! What about that new store Kelly was talking about? What's it called . . . MacDougal's?"

"Yeah—MacDougal's! I think I saw it over near Lamm's."

We headed in that direction. I tried not to think about my fight with Bailey. I mean, since when was *he* in charge of *me*?

I followed Jody into the new store. A jukebox was playing in one corner. There were strings of lights hanging from the ceiling. Rock band posters covered the walls. Loud music pounded from the speakers.

"I love it!" Jody shouted over the noise. "Don't you?"

"Yeah!" I'd never seen anything like it. What a cool store.

Jody picked up an outrageous pair of bright green shoes with platform heels. "They're me!"

"Definitely," I answered.

We cruised the aisles, listening to the music. I started to feel better. Forget about Bailey, I told myself. He just doesn't get it.

Jody stopped at one of the racks. She pulled out a long-sleeved knit shirt with stripes across the chest. "Don't you love this? I saw it in the window."

I did love it. A lot. "It's great."

Jody kept holding the shirt. She danced around to the music. Then she pulled an identical one from the rack. "Here, Claud. We should both get one—then we'll have matching shirts."

She handed the shirt to me. I couldn't stop staring at it. I liked the idea of matching shirts. It would show how Jody and I are best friends. Without Kelly.

Jody glanced around the store. Then she slid the shirt off the hanger and stuffed it under her jacket. She kept moving to the music.

I held the other shirt hanger in my hand. I knew what Jody wanted me to do. And it would be easy to take the shirt. Jody already got away with it. No one even saw her.

I thought about Bailey. How he wouldn't listen to me. It would serve him right if I took the shirt.

I eased the shirt off the hanger.

And then I stopped.

What am I doing? I thought. How can I do this again? It's just . . . wrong. I remembered Bailey's words. How he said I was immature. Stupid.

I glanced over at Jody. "Come *on,*" she whispered.

Bailey was right. It *was* immature and stupid. I could get caught, and it would affect my whole family. I wanted to have a matching shirt with Jody. But not enough to put my family on the line.

And Bailey wasn't trying to boss me around. He was just watching out for me. He didn't want to see me get in trouble.

Jody danced closer to me. "Hurry up," she whispered. "I can't hang around much longer with this thing under my jacket."

I shook my head. "I can't take it."

"Why not? No one's looking."

"No, I mean I can't shoplift anymore," I said. "Sorry."

Jody frowned. "Don't you want matching shirts?"

"Yes! I really do, Jody. But I just can't *steal* it. It's wrong."

Jody stared at me. She looked really bummed. "I thought you were into this now, Claud," she said.

"I'm sorry," I told her.

"Well, you should be," she snapped. "Because now we can't have matching shirts."

How could I explain it to her? I mean, I probably

wanted those matching shirts as much as Jody. But I wasn't going to steal ever again—no matter how much I wanted to.

"Jody, I want to hang out and have fun with you. And I want matching shirts," I said. "But after Shannon got caught, I just started thinking. You know, about my family. If I got caught stealing, we would *all* be in big trouble."

Jody rolled her eyes.

"It's just . . . stealing is wrong. I don't *need* any of this stuff," I tried to explain. "And my parents taught me not to steal. I can't just take something that doesn't belong to me."

Jody didn't say anything.

"It doesn't mean I'm not your best friend," I told her. "If I had money, I would buy us matching shirts."

Jody shrugged and turned her back to me.

I knew she was mad. She might even be mad enough to drop me as her best friend. But what could I do? If she wanted me to do something I thought was wrong, I guess we couldn't be best friends.

But still, I think Jody understands me more than she likes to admit. I had a feeling she would stay my best friend no matter what.

"I'll call you later," I said.

She didn't look up. She just pulled the shirt out from under her jacket and dropped it on the floor.

"Later," she said.

I headed out into the mall and walked toward the bus stop. What am I going to do about Bailey? I wondered. What if he told Charlie and Julia?

It doesn't matter, I realized. Because if Bailey didn't tell them, *I* will. My shoplifting could have hurt the whole family. So the whole family deserves to know about it.

I felt better as I climbed back onto the bus. I'll tell the truth, I thought. I stole things, and I knew it was wrong, and I brought them back.

Mom and Dad would be proud of me.

I was proud of myself.

YOU COULD WIN A TRIP TO SEE WHERE THEY FILM

party of five™

GRAND PRIZE
A weekend (4 days/3 nights) trip to Los Angeles, CA, including a tour of the Sony Pictures Entertainment, Inc. studio lot

5 FIRST PRIZES
Party of Five sweatshirt

15 SECOND PRIZES
Party of Five baseball hat

25 THIRD PRIZES
Party of Five T-Shirt

50 FOURTH PRIZES
Party of Five mug

Minstrel® Books
Published by Pocket Books

COLUMBIA PICTURES TELEVISION
a SONY PICTURES ENTERTAINMENT company

Complete the entry form and send to:
Pocket Books/"Party of Five" Sweepstakes
Advertising and Promotion Department
1230 Avenue of the Americas, New York, NY 10020

Name_____ Birthdate___/___/___

Address_____

City_____ State_____ Zip_____

Phone(____) _____

See Back for official rules   1296 (1 of 2)

"Party of Five" SWEEPSTAKES Official Rules

1. No Purchase Necessary. Enter by mailing the completed Official Entry Form (no copies allowed) or by mailing on a 3" x 5" card with your name and address, daytime telephone number and birthdate to the Pocket Books/"Party of Five" Sweepstakes, Advertising and Promotion Department, 13th Floor, 1230 Avenue of the Americas, NY, NY 10020. Entries must be received by 6/30/97. Not responsible for lost, late, damaged, stolen, illegible, mutilated, incomplete, or misdirected or not delivered entries or mail or for typographical errors in the entry form or rules. Entries are void if they are in whole or in part illegible, incomplete or damaged. Enter as often as you wish, but each entry must be mailed separately. Winners will be selected at random from all eligible entries received in a drawing to be held on or about 7/1/97. Winners will be notified by mail.

2. Prizes: One Grand Prize: A weekend (four days/three nights) trip for up to four persons (the winning minor, one parent or legal guardian and two guests) including round-trip coach airfare from the major U.S. airport nearest the winner's residence, ground transportation or car rental, meals, three nights in a hotel (one room, occupancy for four) and a tour of the Sony Pictures Entertainment studio lot in Culver City, CA *(approx. retail value $3500.00)*, Five First Prizes: "Party of Five" sweatshirts *(approx. retail value $30 each)* Fifteen Second Prizes: "Party of Five" baseball caps *(approx. retail value $16.00 each)* , Twenty-five Third Prizes: "Party of Five" T-shirts *(approx. retail value $15.00 each)*. Fifty Fourth Prizes: "Party of Five" mugs *(approx. retail value: $7.50 each)*. The Grand Prize must be taken on the dates specified by sponsors. Sony Pictures Entertainment, Inc. in its sole discretion may substitute another prize for the studio tour if such tour can no longer be offered.

3. The sweepstakes is open to legal residents of the U.S. and Canada (excluding Quebec) no older than fourteen as of 6/30/97, except as set forth below. Proof of age is required to claim prize. Prizes will be awarded to the winner's parent or legal guardian. Any minor taking a Grand Prize trip must be accompanied by a parent or legal guardian. Grand Prize winner, winner's parent or legal guardian and guests must submit a Release of Liability Publicity Release prior to ticketing. Void in Puerto Rico and wherever else prohibited or restricted by law. All federal, state and local laws apply. Sony Pictures Entertainment, Inc., Columbia Pictures Television, Inc., Simon & Schuster, Inc., Parachute Press, Inc., their officers, directors, shareholders, employees, suppliers, parents, subsidiaries, affiliates, agencies, sponsors, participating retailers, and persons connected with the use, marketing or conduct of this sweepstakes are not eligible. And family members living in the same household as any of the individuals referred to in the immediately forgoing sentence are not eligible.

4. One prize per person or household. Prizes are not transferable and may not be substituted except by sponsors, in event of unavailability, in which case a prize of equal or greater value will be awarded. All prizes will be awarded. The odds of winning a prize depend upon the number of eligible entries received.

5. If a winner is a Canadian resident, then he/she must correctly answer a skill-based question administered by mail.

6. All expenses on receipt and use of prize including federal, state and local taxes are the sole responsibility of the winners. Winners will be notified by mail. Winners may be required to execute and return an Affidavit of Eligibility and Release and all other legal documents which the sweepstakes sponsor may require (including a W-9 tax form) within 15 days of attempted notification or an alternate winner will be selected.

7. Winners or winners' parents on winners' behalf agree to allow use of their names, photographs, likenesses, and entries for any advertising, promotion and publicity purposes without further compensation to or permission from the entrants, except where prohibited by law.

8. Winners agree that Sony Pictures Entertainment, Inc., Columbia Pictures Television, Inc., Simon & Schuster, Inc., Parachute Press, Inc., their officers, directors, shareholders, employees, suppliers, parents, subsidiaries, affiliates, agencies, sponsors, participating retailers, and persons connected with the use, marketing or conduct of this sweepstakes, shall have no responsibility or liability for injuries, losses or damages of any kind in connection with the collection, acceptance or use of the prizes awarded herein, or from participation in this promotion. By participating in this sweepstakes, participants agree to release, discharge and hold harmless Sony Pictures Entertainment, Inc., Columbia Pictures Television, Inc., Simon & Schuster, Inc., Parachute Press, Inc., their officers, directors, shareholders, employees, suppliers, parents, subsidiaries, affiliates, agencies, sponsors, participating retailers, and persons connected with the use, marketing or conduct of this sweepstakes from any injuries, losses or damages of any kind arising out of the acceptance, use, misuse or possession of any prize received in this sweepstakes.

9. By participating in this sweepstakes, entrants agree to be bound by these rules and the decisions of the judges and sweepstakes sponsors, which are final in all matters relating to the sweepstakes.

10. For a list of major prize winners, (available after 7/5/97) send a stamped, self-addressed envelope to Prize Winners, Pocket Books/"Party of Five" Sweepstakes, Advertising and Promotion Department, 13th Floor, 1230 Avenue of the Americas, NY, NY 10020. "Party of Five" and the "Party of Five" logo are trademarks of Columbia Pictures Television, Inc. No celebrity endorsement implied. © 1997 Columbia Pictures Television, Inc. All rights reserved.